MW00980431

RUN TRUE

A novel by John Fewster

Copyright © 2018 John Fewster

ISBN: 978-0-9919358-2-6

1st Edition

Publisher: Policeman's Creek Publishing

All rights reserved. This book may not be reproduced, stored in a retrieval system, or transmitted, in any form or by any means, electronic, mechanical, photocopying, recording or otherwise, in whole or in part, without written permission from the author, except by reviewer, who may quote brief passages in a review.

This novel is a work of fiction. Names, characters, businesses, events and incidents appearing in this work are fictitious. Any resemblance to real persons, living or dead, is purely coincidental.

Writing a novel requires the support of a village. Thank you to the following villagers for their help:

Fred McCall and Dixie McCall for their love and encouragement.

Tracy Fewster, who provided insightful observations and advice during the writing of this novel, for believing that all things are possible, for her continued patience, and without whom this novel would not exist.

Wayne McEachern for contributing to the inspiration for this novel and for taking time out of his demanding schedule to provide great review comments.

Shannon Fewster and Sarah Fewster for finding time in their hectic lives to offer valuable feedback.

Susan E. Smith for her encouragement and for holding the Sunday Brunch group together; the glue that preserves the village.

Table of Contents

Open Arms

Borj sleeps while the scattered light of a false dawn peers tenuously into the night sky.

Next to his foldaway bed, a radio-alarm clock squats on the floor. Electrons whir in the clock's computer chip silently counting the earth's transit through 360 degrees of daily rotary motion. Another earth-grinding minute passes into history.

'7:14,' the clock confidently proclaims.

'Drip, drip' counter the water drops, escaping from the kitchen tap.

'7:15,' announces the clock. The alarm steals electrons to power the radio speaker.

"Hey people of Lore, wake up!" demands the radio announcer in a burst of static. "It's Max Hammer time with yours truly. It's a chilly fall morning in the city," Max notes. "Don't forget the Independence Rally tonight at the Inspire Megadome in honor of this great country of ours, Freeforall. The rally will be followed by a matchup between the Millhouse Guardians and the Coldstream Rebels. Tonight's game is sponsored by Clear Call Communications, a division of Millhouse Enterprises. Remember, when you need information, Clear Call Communications gives you what you need when you need it. Now let's give a listen to Simon and Garfunkel's *The Boxer*."

The radio bombards the tinny speaker with electrons, creating a pale imitation of the song with scarcely enough strength to fill the one-room apartment.

1

An arm automatically slides out from under the covers and swings horizontally away from the bed. Like the boom on a tower crane with its precision gears and cables, the action of the arm is smooth and effortless. It stops, having precisely suspended a hand in midair above a predetermined point. The arm relaxes. Gravity pulls. The hand drops, hitting the alarm's off-button.

'mum...' sings the speaker, cut off in mid-word.

The arm rises and retracts.

Throwing off his covers, Borj swings his legs out and then down in tandem and counter to the mass of his upper body. All motion stops when his feet contact the cold floor, his slumped body having achieved a sitting position along a more-or-less vertical axis. He rubs his face and bleary eyes.

The clock dutifully and silently persists, counting the milliseconds.

Shuddering against the clammy cold of his T-shirt, Borj gathers himself for the day.

The T-shirt was part of his costume from last year's staff Halloween party at the National Protection Agency, NPA, where Borj works as a superhero. The NPA office manager, Clayton Pitts, who is not a superhero, announced that there would be prizes for best costume. He divided the superheroes into teams to encourage a friendly competition. The theme of the party was 'Escape into Danger'.

Borj and his team members played it conservatively, wearing prison uniforms with 'Property of Millhouse Correctional Institution' stenciled on the front of each T-shirt.

The Alice in Wonderland team won.

All the employees had a good time except for P-Cut (aka: Paper-Cut-Man), who, at the time, was a superhero. P-Cut was arrested while walking home in costume at 3 a.m. The arresting officer believed that P-Cut was an escapee from the local correctional facility named after the founding father of the city of Lore, Cyrus Caesar Millhouse.

The Millhouse family motto was and still is 'Building the Truth Shall Set You Free'. To this end, Cyrus, at the request of the government of the day, built the first privately owned and run prison facility in the then newly incorporated Greater District of Pelmelbound. Cyrus believed that through atonement an inmate could acquire truth and thereby repent for his or her waywardness. Redemption required harsh, character-building lessons, which Cyrus was more than willing to help facilitate for the good of the errant souls and the community. The institution is known locally as 'The Millhouse'.

Using the money earned from the construction and on-going revenue generated by the prison, Cyrus built the first flour mill in the district. 'The Flour Mill', became the cornerstone for Millhouse Enterprises (ME), a fully integrated agribusiness that focused on wheat and other grains. Under the stewardship of his offspring, ME continued to grow. It became an international conglomerate that today spans many facets of commerce, including farming, mining, manufacturing, construction, transportation, banking, communication and pharmaceuticals, to name only a handful. ME prospered and so too did Lore, turning into the administrative headquarters for all things ME. Many of the Millhouse commercial ventures still dominate the city skyline.

Borj runs his hands uneasily through his hair. He had a recurring dream last night. In his dream, he stood on a wharf in the black of night. On the opposite side of a bay was a steel mill with its monolithic towers, enormous blast furnaces, and immense rolling mills housed in cavernous structures. The distant thunder of clashing metal exploded from the buildings as though someone was tossing diesel locomotives in a game of dice. The mill changed into a monstrous, mechanical being with arms and legs. It slowly rose to dominate even the night, and strode across the bay toward Borj. The bay was no more than a puddle to the colossus. The relentless grating of metal-on-metal was deafening. The machine looked down at Borj. The heat from its gigantic blast-furnace eyes was almost unbearable. The monster reached for Borj with a hand the size of a house. Borj awoke in panic. After half an hour of tossing and turning, he fell into a restless sleep.

Borj takes a deep breath and slowly exhales.

Maybe a quiet day at NPA, no surprises, he speculates. *Yeah, like that'll happen. Don't super villains take vacations?*

'7:30. Get up.' the clock demands.

'Drip.' The sound of a rebellious waterdrop leaks into the dark.

Orienting his body on his X, Y and Z axes, Borj rises, locating himself above his feet. He shuffles across the unvarnished floor, worn down by the countless feet of previous tenants, and inserts himself into a closet-sized bathroom.

A hand flails in midair. It's searching for the elusive chain that dangles from a light-bulb socket suspended from the ceiling by a fraying electrical cord. Finally, the hand grasps the chain and pulls. A harsh brilliance leaps into the room. Automatically Borj's eyes shutter to slits. The incandescent light bulb swings erratically overhead, performing a herky-jerky dance. The intensity camouflages shapes in a broken pattern of light and shadow. Nothing is what it seems. Unforgiving brightness leaks fitfully into the apartment through the partially open bathroom doorway. On the far wall opposite the bathroom, the escaping beam intermittently illuminates a picture hanging askew on an otherwise bare wall. If you look closely at the picture in the turbulent light, you can see a yellowing newspaper photo. Attired in his superhero outfit, Borj is accepting the key to the city of Lore for his outstanding work in the fight against super villains. He wears a big smile.

In the bathroom, Borj tilts forward slightly, propping his head against the sloped wall formed by the inclined pitch of the roof that squeezes the walls of his upper-floor apartment.

'Squeak, squeak,' complain the resisting sink taps. The faint sound of running water trickles into the apartment. He splashes water on his face, washing away the remnants of last night's dream. The wall relinquishes support for Borj's head when he turns his attention to the stubble on his face. With a disposable razor in hand, he stoops and squints at a broken mirror propped against the sink. In accordance with the laws of physics, the light bulb begins to settle down, swinging dully from its cord in its now mildly erratic dance. Borj moves from side to side in time with the movement of the bulb, maneuvering for position within his cramped confines. He bobs and weaves, catching glimpses of his opponent in the mirror: a montage of eye, chin, throat, cheek, ear and nose. Finished, he wipes his face with a fragment of frayed towel and tosses it in the sink.

He turns off the light, throwing the bathroom once again into darkness. The unseen light bulb leaps about with renewed energy.

The sun begins its ascent. Light inches across the earth, revealing the brickwork in narrow canyons carved by the jumble of buildings that make up the city. Through a series of miraculous twists and turns, the feeble dawn creeps through the narrow, north-facing window that is Borj's portal on an alley. Windows of the facing buildings lining the alley stare back unknowingly. He flicks on a light switch.

Borj fills a pot with water and places it on a two-element hotplate. After a quick rinse of an NPA cup liberated from his workplace, he spoons in instant coffee; pours in boiling water; and adds a scoop of coffee creamer. He tosses a couple of slices of day-old bread onto the hotplate.

He turns on an ancient TV that rests on a sturdy cardboard box. The vertical hold on the TV is going. Borj whacks the side of it to coax a stable picture.

'Hey! What's that for? Knock it off will ya!' protests the TV before deciding to cooperate.

Satisfied with the result, Borj sits down.

"The latest census figures are out and it doesn't look good for Lore," begins TV news anchor, Sam Knoasee. "Figures indicate an ongoing, steep decline in human capital as the populace continues to leave the city in ever-increasing numbers. Loreans are departing to seek employment in New Grubbeemitts where an economic boom is taking place in the nearby coalfields. New Grubbeemitts is a city in the remote country of Pawsoff. When asked to comment, the Mayor of Lore had this to say in an interview with our lead reporter Will Icantseeh, who is standing by on the steps of city hall. Will, over to you."

"Sam, the mayor talked about the impact of the diminishing population," begins Will.

A clip from the interview commences.

"The drop in human capital is negatively impacting the tax base," affirms Mayor Mack Row. "The resulting precipitous deterioration in the city's revenue makes it increasingly difficult to maintain infrastructure. Cutbacks to municipal services are ongoing. School closings persist due to a declining client base. Manufacturers are closing their facilities in Lore and moving their operations to Pawsoff to better service their new clientele. The problem is exacerbated by national and local retailers closing their doors. Retail closures are the result of market forces adversely affecting the bottom line. Lore is becoming financially unviable."

"Will, is there anything more you can tell us?"

"I did attempt to talk to city councillor Ive Gotmyne, a strong opponent of the mayor's plan to reverse the economic decay. The councillor was unavailable. Currently he is on a fact-finding mission in Pawsoff. In a related item,

6

a job fair sponsored by Millhouse Mining Ltd, a subsidiary of Millhouse Enterprises, is looking for workers for its mining operations in New Grubbeemitts. The job fair runs this Saturday and Sunday at the Inspire Megadome, a division of Clear Call Communications. Back to you Sam."

"Thanks, Will. In other news, a meteor was sighted north of the city in the predawn hours. The meteor lit up the sky as it plummeted to earth. There are no reports of damage."

"In international news, coal miners in New Grubbeemitts are staging work stoppages and mass rallies to protest…"

'Fire! Fire!' shrieks a smoke detector.

"Shit!" curses Borj, leaping up to rescue his burning toast. He grabs his superhero cape on the bed and beats the toast, knocking the slices to the floor. The flames die out after a couple of swats. Scooping up the slices, he tosses them on the kitchen counter.

He quickly opens the window. Cool air floods in. The smoke begins to dissipate. The smoke detector stops.

"…Pawsoff gained its independence three years ago after three-hundred years of colonial rule by Greatland," Sam Knoasee reports. "Since gaining independence, there has been ongoing political unrest resulting from the dichotomy between the two major political parties, the Tories and the Neoconservatives. Both parties are vying for control of the Open House, the main legislative body of Pawsoff."

Borj turns off the TV.

The inevitable is gaining momentum. The apartment hallway comes to life with the familiar thunder of approaching footsteps. News travels fast, and with it a response as predictable as the movement of the earth.

'Bang, bang, bang! Someone to see you,' the apartment door announces cheerfully.

"Hey!" shouts the booming voice of the building superintendent, Frank, in summons to the alarm. "Hey! Are

7

ya cooking in there? Ya know ya aren't supposed to. Ya got a hotplate? This isn't a five-star hotel. If ya want first class, go uptown. What's going on in there? Open up!"

'Bang, bang, bang! Hello! There's someone to see you. It sounds urgent and he's angry. Better deal with it,' cautions the door. 'Make something up. Use your imagination.'

Borj picks up a slice of toast and takes a bite.

'Crrrrrrch, crrrrrrch…' The sound of the toast's cinder crunchiness fills the apartment.

"Hey! Are ya in there? I'm talking to ya," hollers Frank. "If I have to break down this door, you're paying for the damage."

"It's okay," Borj shouts, between mouthfuls of toast. "Everything is alright. It was the clothes iron. I left it on too long; burned my tights. I was pressing them; forgot I had the iron on."

"Tights! Since when do ya iron tights? Open up! I want to see what's going on in there!"

'Bang, bang, bang! Hey! Deal with this guy, will ya?' the door pleads. 'I can't take much more of this.'

"It's all right," Borj yells. "It's under control. I opened the window. The smoke will clear in a second."

"Your rent is three-days overdue. If ya don't pay up, you'll find your crap out on the street. I have to answer to Millhouse Enterprises and they want to tear down this dump. The Open Arms Apartments isn't a retirement home for has-been superheroes. Is this sinking in?"

"Yeah, I know. I'll get the money."

"When?"

"Soon."

"Soon isn't good enough! I want it by the end of the week or you're out on your ass."

"I hear ya," replies Borj, unsure where he will get the money. He has already pawned his superhero weapon.

"All right then, end of the week or you're out. There are bills to pay. Carrying ya doesn't pay the bills. Ya got that super guy?"

"Yeah, I got it."

"Enough said." There is the sound of righteous footsteps receding down the hallway.

The door is silent on the matter.

Borj munches on his second piece of toast. Finished, he rinses down his breakfast with coffee.

He fishes a pair of black tights from a laundry hamper and carefully pulls them on, so as not to rip them. Recently, he has put on a little weight. Next, he slides on his tattered, sunrise-orange, superhero shorts and shirt that have endured many battles against the super villains who plague the city. He laces on his tatty, calf-high, red-leather, wrestling boots. Before donning his frayed sunrise-orange cape, Borj brushes away the evidence of burnt toast. Emblazoned on the cape is a large, slightly crooked 'B' that Borj had to sew on because he couldn't afford to pay his tailor. The B looks like this.

He looks at himself in a full-length mirror and is troubled by the result, as though not comfortable in his own skin. He adjusts his costume to little avail.

Alien?

Closing his apartment door, Borj secures it with several locks. Even superheroes aren't immune to break-ins. He stashes the keys in one of the many pockets sewn to the inside of his cape.

The dimly lit hallway is empty except for a man leaning against a wall. Borj doesn't recognize him and pays little attention. Tenant turnover is high from week to week. The itinerant's head is buried behind an early edition of the daily newspaper, the Lickspittle Free Press.

The paper, with its reliance on advertising revenue, is not a clarion call for freedom of the press in the way 'Free' suggests. The Lickspittle is free in the sense that you don't have to pay for it. This is the marketing strategy adopted by the Liberty Guard Corp. Ltd. (LGC), which owns the paper and many sister publications in the Greater District of Pelmelbound. The free newspaper garners lots of eyeballs. The marketing strategy also deters rival corporations from setting up shop. LGC is a subsidiary of Clear Call Communications.

Passing the tenant, Borj glances at the morning headline splashed across the front page: Alien Crashes North of Lore. Dredged from the archives of the Lickspittle, the likeness of an archetypical extraterrestrial appears beneath the headline.

A bald, middle-aged head with alien-looking symbols tattooed on its forehead emerges above the paper. A man peers warily at Borj through a pair of thick-rimmed, retro, bug-eye glasses. Recognizing Borj's uniform, a look of astonishment crosses his angular face.

"Hey, aren't ya that Borj guy?" he says, pronouncing the 'j' in Borj.

"It's Borj. The 'j' is silent," answers Borj without stopping.

"Have ya seen this morning's headline? It says an alien crash-landed outside Lore. Ya seen the picture?" The tenant holds up the paper to the quickly receding Borj. "Says it could be the start of the Apocalypse. Ya going to fight this guy?"

"No," Borj answers confidently with the authority of one who is in the know.

"Why not? That's what they pay ya for."

"It's a meteorite, nothing more."

Wanting to avoid the jaundiced eyes of the apartment superintendent, who will be entrenched behind his desk in the main lobby, Borj elects to take the stairs leading to a side entrance that ejects him into an alley. He heads to the sidewalk in front of the building. The once busy street is almost deserted.

He walks toward the subway station where he will catch the southbound 8:15. Unable to resist, he stops for a minute in front of a pawnshop. There are the usual items in the window: musical instruments, cameras, etc. The barred window reflects a pale image of Borj. Reluctantly, he walks away.

Scrambles

Borj descends the stairs into the Mandown subway station. A rush of air charges up the stairs to announce the arrival of a train somewhere down below. His cape flaps behind him. At the ticket kiosk, he pays the fare and pushes through the turnstile. He stops with a jerk. His cape is caught. Impatiently, he yanks on it, pulling it free.

Taking the escalator to the catacomb of tunnels, he navigates his way toward the platform. He can hear music bouncing off the white-tiled walls of the station. The subway authority licenses musicians to entertain rush-hour commuters in exchange for whatever spare change the scurrying migrants are willing to cough up. The sound is coming from every direction and growing louder. Borj recognizes the distinctive style of playing. A guitar player materializes as Borj turns a corner. The musician is squeezed into an alcove, only steps from the entrance to the platform. Performers must not impede the efficient flow of commuter traffic.

Borj smiles warmly, recognizing his friend, Scrambles, who is a local legend in the music industry for his unique style of guitar playing and singing. His fingers scramble seemingly unpredictably over frets, chording impossible and surprising combinations of notes. As he strums a tangled cadence, he rushes through the lyrics, and then suddenly lingers over a phrase, often not placing the emphasis where you might expect. Somehow the whole thing flows, like that's the way it should always be.

Scrambles howls the lyrics to *Takin' Care of Business*. He smiles at Borj and nods in recognition of a fellow musician. Borj stops to listen while keeping an eye on the train platform.

"Hey Borj," greets Scrambles, strumming his guitar to the song.

"Hey, where have ya been? Haven't seen ya."

"Subway robocracy did a spit-take; pulled my license. One of the tube people took exception to one of my songs. He complained. Course the robocracy said the song wasn't appropriate, even though they never listened to it."

"Must've touched a nerve. What's the song?"

"*Errand Boy*."

"Don't know that one. Who wrote it?"

"Yours truly," Scrambles says proudly with a smile. "Based it on a line from a movie, *Apocalypse Now*. Ya know it? This guy, Colonel Kurtz, tells Captain Willard—he's the hero of the story—that Willard is a stooge sent to collect a bill. Calls Willard an errand boy. Says he was sent by a bunch of grocery clerks. Kurtz nails it. Ya should see it." Inspired, Scrambles plays a few bars.

"Sounds promising. I'd like to hear more. Maybe ya can play it for me sometime."

"I got a gig at a bar called Inside the Whale. Ya know it? Drop by. I'll play it for ya. Hey! Bring your sax, do a little jamming like the old days. Those were good times."

"I pawned my sax," Borj admits, feeling ashamed. "Need to eat."

On hearing the news, Scrambles stops playing. "That's not good," he says, shaking his head in disbelief. "Never thought that would happen. You and that sax…" Absent-mindedly, he resumes strumming *Takin' Care of Business*, only now it sounds like a dirge.

"It happens. I'll get it back."

"Yeah, that's right. You'll get it back." Scramble smiles uncertainly.

"Anyway, you're here now," says Borj." How's it going?"

"Not good. There are a lot fewer ears down here these days." He picks up the tempo on his guitar and wails a couple of lines as inducement to a passing specter, who tosses a few coins into an open guitar case. "Thank you," shouts Scrambles, responding to the generosity of the rapidly disappearing apparition. "Things are slow," says Scrambles, strumming his guitar. "It's like this all over Lore," he adds, with a nod of his head at the diminishing crowd. "This time of day, they used to be packed in here like soda crackers. Now they're disappearing fast. I'm thinking of moving on; nothing to keep me here. I hear there's good money in a place called New Grubbeemitts. Ya know it? Ya think they got a subway there?"

"Don't know."

"What about you? Ya interested? New Grubbeemitts I mean."

"No, don't think so."

"Ya sure? Not much left here. City's dying. Maybe ya should think on it."

Scrambles plays louder as a potential philanthropist walks by. He ignores the guitar case.

"How are things going at superhero central?"

The wind rushes into the station announcing the arrival of Borj's train.

"Could be better. My ride's here. I've got to go," he says with a nod in the direction of the platform. "I'll see ya." Borj turns and hustles over to the train.

"Don't forget Inside the Whale," yells Scrambles at the vanishing Borj.

Scrambles wails and strums feverishly at the passing ears, hoping for a few more crumbs of largesse to fill his shrinking larder.

The doors slide shut behind Borj. The train shudders and picks up speed.

A few late comers hustle onto the platform. Some are annoyed, having missed the departing train. Others simply shrug it off.

Borj watches Scrambles through a window. Jerking and swaying to his music, Scrambles howls at the newly arrived commuters. He bangs home the last few chords for a big finish.

"Yeah!" hollers Scrambles as the last train car exits the station.

Drifton

Borj relaxes in his seat. He glances at the dull-eyed subway passengers with their far-away look. Like his companion commuters, he's careful not to make eye contact.

With little else to do, Borj turns his attention to the advertising that festoons the car. A new movie, *The Dropout*, is playing to mixed reviews. Many reviewers are perplexed by the title because no one seems to have dropped out of anything; everything seems normal. Elsewhere, there's an ad for an edgy travel magazine called *New Seekers and Travelers*. The ad features the cover of the latest edition of the magazine with a picture of a successful middle-aged couple. Standing on an ocean cliff, they are dressed for North Atlantic whale watching. In the distance, a whale breaches.

The train dumps Borj at the Drifton station. The station is named after Nicholas Drifton, who is known as Nickels in mining circles. Nickels was an example of a local boy who, through hard work and entrepreneurial spirit, made good, becoming the CEO of an international mining conglomerate, Millhouse Mining Ltd. His career was interrupted after the Freeforall government revealed that Nickels was illegally shipping military weapons to support the embattled powers-that-be in Pawsoff. The Freeforall administration had for many years ignored Nickel's assistance, until Pawsoff's Prime Minister, Geht Lawst, ran afoul of Nickels' government. Lawst shifted his country's allegiance to an alternate trading block. The authorities insisted on numerous occasions that Nickels end his backing. Nickels persisted. Mining in Pawsoff is very lucrative.

After sentencing, Nickels shrugged and stated, "All of us find ourselves on the wrong side of the law now and then."

By the time of his sentencing, the subway station had been built, named after Nickels and in use for several years. Many of his detractors tried to have the station renamed. However, even after sentencing, Nickels had his defenders, who admired his go-get-em attitude. They successfully rallied to quell the name change by invoking the prohibitive cost, which was deemed an outrageous burden to taxpayers.

Nickels currently resides in The Millhouse. Now head of the inmates' entertainment committee, he is currently organizing the production of a musical play, *Makes the World Go Around*, which he wrote and stars in. The Millhouse correctional staff lauds Nickels for his exemplary leadership, organizational skills, and commercial acumen. He is a strong candidate for early parole. Nickels plans to run for political office after his release. There are appalling federal laws that hobble legitimate commercial interests on the international stage.

As for Lawst, he was deposed in an uprising that was presented in the media as a revolt by the common people. The country's new leader, Colonel Squashem, promises democratic reform sometime in the future. Fleeing the country, the former Prime Minister found refuge in the country of Saemolstory. Aided by a consortium of international banks, Lawst lives very comfortably in exile, having had the foresight before his political demise to create a rainy-day fund using money appropriated from the Pawsoff Treasury.

Borj's thoughts turn to the coming workday as he rides the subway escalator. He's concerned about the best way to approach his boss, Clay, with a request for an advance on his salary to pay the overdue rent.

17

What do I say to him? he wonders. *Hi Clay, my rent is due. Can I get an advance against next week's pay? That's too abrupt. Maybe wait for an opening. Sure as shit, he'll launch into his fiscal responsibility speech the minute I ask. How much do I ask for? Maybe if I...*

Borj's thought is cut short when the escalator yanks him back as he steps off.

'Hey! Where do ya think you're going?' the escalator demands. 'I'm not done with ya. Come here. I'll tell ya when ya can go.'

Borj's cape is caught. He reaches for the emergency stop, but can't reach it. Things are moving fast. He's pulled down onto his knees. He can hear people shouting. Grabbing his cape, he pulls hard. It rips cleanly along a perforated edge. Fortunately, his former tailor foresaw the likelihood of entanglement. She created a cape with rows of perforations, much like those in a role of paper toweling. He watches while the bottom third of his cape disappears into the escalator's maw.

A hand hits a stop button.

"Ya okay buddy?" asks a man standing next to Borj. "That thing almost ate ya for breakfast. Here, let me help ya up."

Shaken, Borj gets up. Others have gathered around.

"I'm okay. Thanks. That was close."

"You're damn right it was close! Holy crap you're lucky!" adds the fellow traveler, examining Borj with the practiced eye of a healthcare worker. "Ya sure you're all right? Ya want to sit down?"

"No, I'm good. Thanks."

The crowd begins to disperse. A few shake their heads in disbelief at the close call.

"Ya should report that!" continues the concerned citizen.

"It was my fault. I wasn't paying attention. The cape was too long. I know I'm supposed to hold it up. I forgot. I had other things on my mind."

"What kind of cape is that anyway? It sure tore evenly. Ya should sit down. Ya want a drink of water?"

"No, I'm good. Thanks."

Borj pulls the cape around in front to see how much is left. "Not likely it'll get caught now." He smiles weakly, knowing how close he came.

"I can wait, if ya need someone to stay with ya."

"I'm okay."

"Be careful next time," the stranger cautions, giving Borj a friendly pat on the shoulder.

Who?

Borj enters a nondescript building. At the far end of a long narrow hallway, stand two stone-faced security officers wearing standard-issue sunglasses and dark suits. Their hands are clasped quietly in front of them. Framed between them, is a baby-poop-yellow door. Painted on the cinder-block wall above the door are the letters 'NPA T3'.

Walking toward the officers, Borj nods at an antiquated man in a small booth crammed into the wall. A sliding glass panel is his window to the wider world presented by the hallway. 'Cornelius', announces the name badge on his shirt. He is dressed in khaki-green, work shirt and pants and wears electric-ultramarine running shoes with neon-green laces. He has propped his feet on the desk that consumes most of his office space. Smoke from his cigarillo seeps out of the cubicle. Despite the cramped conditions, he appears relaxed. Cornelius turns the page of his Lickspittle Free Press. 'God Raptures Local Businessman!' shouts a headline. He chuckles, ignoring Borj, who continues on his journey.

"Morning guys," says Borj with a smile, as he approaches the security guards.

The guards are considered overhead, a necessary evil that is part of the cost of doing business. The agency introduced them several years ago to protect NPA facilities against super villains (SVs) and disgruntled civilians. An altercation between a superhero and an SV often results in damage and loss of personal property. A clash can decimate an entire city block, leading to claims of negligence against a superhero. The city of Lore does not cover the cost. Loreans can buy insurance to protect their property. Few do. The cost is prohibitive and there is an avalanche of paperwork when submitting an insurance claim. To avoid court-ordered judgments for restitution, many superheroes spend countless hours in court defending their actions. NPA does not cover time spent in courtrooms. Superheroes, who can afford it, carry insurance. Borj does not. The courts are sympathetic toward superheroes. Nevertheless, the courts must deal fairly with each claimant. Being a superhero is a tough business.

Borj reaches for the door handle. Barr, one of the security guards, gently lays a hand on Borj's arm.

"Did ya forget something?" Barr asks, without looking at Borj.

"What?"

"Your security badge, your ID."

"Ah ya must be kidding!" fumes Borj. He fumbles in his cape for his ID. "Really, my security badge? Who else would dress like this in this neighborhood?"

"Can't let ya in without it. Those are the rules. Maybe you're an SV or a civilian dressed to look like Borj, so ya can infiltrate the premises. We don't know. Can't take any chances. This is for your security too."

"I come in here every day. Ya know me as well as I know myself."

After rummaging in his cape, Borj realizes his badge was eaten by the escalator.

"I don't have it," says Borj. His frustration is beginning to show.

"If ya need a temporary badge, talk to the fossil."

"The fossil?"

"Yeah, ya know, what's his name, the guy in the security booth," says Barr with a jerk of his head in Cornelius' direction. "Ya know the drill."

ID'd

Borj stands patiently in front of the glass panel, waiting to be noticed.

Cornelius is engrossed in his newspaper. 'Unidentified Man Taken into Custody' announces a headline. Beneath the article is a half-page advertisement cautioning Loreans about identity theft and where to buy protection. 'Don't let someone steal your identity. Protect yourself. Get protection today. To learn more, visit http://millhouse_enterprises.com/identity/theft'.

Finally, with no response, Borj taps on the glass panel.

Annoyed, the old guy looks up from his paper. He gives the impression of one who feels unjustly tormented. He squints at Borj.

"What?" is the muffled reply through the glass partition.

"I lost my ID, my security badge. I need a new one."

"What? Speak up. I can't hear ya," barks Cornelius. Inwardly he chuckles in anticipation of the scene that is about to unfold.

"I lost my badge," shouts Borj. "I need a new one."

Cornelius cups his hand to his ear. Smoke from his cigarillo wafts upward, amalgamating with the foul air above him.

"A badge, I need a badge! ID! Open up will ya!"

Shaking his head in irritation, the diminutive Cornelius extricates himself from his chair. Leaning over his desk, he slides open the glass panel.

"What's up, kid? What did ya say? I'm busy here. What do ya want?"

"The name's Borj, not kid," he corrects firmly. "Can ya give me an ID badge?" He looks at the burning cigarillo that seems permanently attached to Cornelius' hand. "And can ya put that thing out?"

"Sure thing, kid." He stubs out his cigarillo in an ashtray. "Anything to help. Now, what's on your mind?" he asks, staring blankly at Borj.

Borj waits in a kind of stupor standoff. Each of them is waiting for the other to blink.

An overhead fluorescent light flickers in a moment of solidarity with the silence.

"I lost my badge. I need a new one," requests Borj, blinking first. "Can ya give me a new ID, a badge?"

"Oh, is that all? Okay, I can help. There's no need to shout. I'm not deaf. Chillax, it's all good." He smiles reassuringly, revealing his yellowing teeth. "That's what I'm here for. I can give ya a temp badge. Got some ID?"

"Sure."

Borj searches his cape. He produces a library card. It's dirty and badly mauled. It expired several years ago. Confidently he slides the card onto the counter. He smiles, feeling that, somehow, he has bested his opponent.

Cornelius peers doubtfully. He deigns to pick it up for closer examination. A faint smile crosses his thin lips.

"Ya got ID with a pitcher?" he challenges with a sniff of disdain, tossing the pathetic offering onto the counter.

"Pitcher? Do ya mean picture?"

"Yeah, that's what I said, pitcher. Ya know, a driver's license or a passport for instance. It's only natural. Anything that's government issued. Preferably ID from the government with a superhero designation, like a superhero license that tells me ya are who ya say ya are."

"Government doesn't issue anything like that. Can ya imagine the government asking a T1 superhero to apply for a license?"

"What's a T1 anyway?"

"T1 is a top-of-the-line superhero."

"What are you then?"

"T3."

"T3 sounds kind of low on the food chain," Cornelius observes, looking unconvinced by the whole rigmarole of superhero designations.

"It'd be a bureaucratic nightmare trying to assess who is and who isn't a T3," explains Borj, ignoring the insult. "It's not a regulated industry. Anyone can be a superhero. After that it's up to you to promote yourself. Get your picture in the paper to prove who ya are. Ya know, show people ya have what it takes."

Borj glances at the Lickspittle, realizing that his newspaper example wasn't the best choice given the questionable articles in the paper. 'I was Born in the Time of the Apocalypse!' screams a headline.

"The government lets ya be whatever? Relying on the Lickspittle sounds kind of iffy. Whole thing sounds fishy to me. And I don't mean that in a religious way either. Anyway, it doesn't matter a hill of beans. T3 or T1, it's all the same to me."

"The system isn't perfect. What do ya need with ID anyway? Ya know who I am," Borj argues with a look of incredulity.

"Ya have to remember, I'm new here. Only been here a few months. So naturally I need some ID with a pitcher. Rules are rules. Ya should know that. I shouldn't have to tell ya." Cornelius is peeved. He does his best to maintain his professional demeanor.

"What happened to the other guy, the guy ya replaced? What's his name?"

"Him, he went to Pawsoff. He was making good money over there working in a tipple. Ya know what a tipple is? Sorts coal according to size. It's a bejesus machine the size of a football stadium. It's real noisy too. Can't hear yourself think. He got stopped by a cop over there. Didn't have his identity papers with him. Makin' license plates now for the government. They're strict over there, not like here. Maybe they'll deport him. Why, what does it matter?"

"He would have vouched for me, no questions asked."

"The reality is no vouching allowed. It stands to reason."

"What stands to reason?"

"The truth is ya can't trust people, so the guys that run this place don't allow no vouching. Ya want to keep things secure, right?"

Borj thrashes impatiently in the pockets of his cape, groping for his driver's license. Finding it, he places it on the counter with a sense of relief.

Cornelius coughs mildly as he assesses the authenticity of the license. Satisfied, he hunts in a desk drawer and pulls out a request form for a temporary badge. He begins filling in the form.

"Where did ya lose it?"

"Drifton station, I had an altercation with a subway escalator." Borj holds up the remnants of his cape to add plausibility to the story.

"You're not the first. Lucky ya didn't get killed. Capes are a damned nuisance and a work-safety violation. That's my two cents. Did ya have the badge when ya got on?"

"What, the escalator? Yeah, of course. That's where I lost it."

"No, not the escalator, the subway train. When ya got on the train, did ya have it?"

"Yeah, sure."

"Which station?"

"Which station what?"

"Which station did ya get on at? Look, these are simple questions. Cooperate, will ya? The boss says do this and I do it. It's that simple."

Borj hesitates, wanting to preserve some privacy. "Why do ya need that?"

"Need it for my records. It's official business. I can't give ya a badge without it."

Borj continues to hold back.

"I haven't got all day. I got work to do. Come on. Let's go. My coffee's getting cold. What's it going to be?" Cornelius hurriedly whirls his arm in a circular motion to convey a let's-get-this-thing-done urgency.

"Mandown, I got on at the Mandown station."

"Mandown, that's a tough neighborhood. What were ya doing down there?"

"I live there."

"Next of kin?"

Borj wavers.

"Case ya get hurt. It happens in your line of work. Ya aren't invincible," he observes, coughing a little harder.

"Joki."

"Joki, that's a strange name. Got a last name?"

"Nope."

"Ya aren't making this easy, are ya? Relationship?"

"Sister."

"Address and phone number?"

"Don't know. She comes and goes."

Cornelius shakes his head in disbelief.

"Okay, stand over there," he orders, motioning with a flick of his head at a height strip on the wall behind Borj. "I'll take the measure of ya," he chuckles.

There's no response from Borj.

"That was a joke."

Borj stares with a look of incomprehension.

"Never mind. Stand over there."

Borj takes up his position.

"Don't smile. Hold still. Look at the camera."

There's a bright flash of light.

Cornelius examines the resulting picture with a critical eye. "Ya got some red eye and your head's a little tilted. Should be straight up. Close enough. This'll do."

Borj's tormentor retrieves a blank temp badge from one of many scattered carelessly in his desk drawer. He carefully applies the picture to the badge. Next, he takes a date stamp, inks it and slams it onto the picture of Borj's face, smudging the date in the process.

"The ink doesn't take, if ya don't hit it hard." Cornelius smiles, feeling pleased. "I enjoy my work. Makes me feel like I'm contributing to the greater good of..." His thought trails off. He is lost in contemplation. After a minute, he resumes his explanation. "Know what I mean? I got my part to play for better or worse. God knows ya need infrastructure to keep this place going," he notes with an expansive flurry of his stamp-clutching hand. The gesture is intended to include the observable dominion of his booth.

Next, he takes a well-worn 'Approved' stamp and bangs it across the picture, obliterating almost all recognition of the image as that of Borj. Then he stamps 'Temporary', followed by 'Property of NPA'. Finally, the provider of IDs smashes 'CKM' on the picture.

"CKM, that's me, my initials. Adds a personal touch and makes it official."

"What's your full name?"

"Cornelius Krissen Millhouse," he proudly announces. "Taking responsibility is important, right?"

Satisfied with his effort, he slaps the card on the counter, further smudging the ink.

"Here ya go, kid. The ink's still wet. Careful how ya handle it. Sign here." He points with a nicotine-stained finger to the line on the bottom of the badge. "Ya can use the pen on the counter. Ya don't mind if I smoke, do ya?" he asks, seating himself in his chair. "Adds to the moment. What is it about the smell of drying ink on a newly minted temp badge and a good smoke?" He pulls out a cigarillo, lights it and tilts back in his chair.

Borj examines the badge. "My own mother wouldn't recognize me."

"Supposed to be getting a new camera soon. That'll lighten my workload. It's all digital. Auto-magically applies the pitcher, dates it, and everything, the whole shebang in one go. Ya don't even have to sign it. The machine does that for ya. Uses a pitcher kept on file in a database, whatever the hell that is. All ya do is supply your signature once. That's progress for ya. You'll see."

"Be careful. Automation might do ya out of a job."

"I'll always have a job. Ya can count on it."

Cornelius coughs again, only deeper and harder this time.

Borj signs, using the pen secured to the counter by a short length of chain that makes writing tricky.

"Hand it to me, will ya? Let's see how ya did." Cornelius leans forward over his desk and extends his hand. A cloud of smoke has reconstituted itself above the old dragon. Borj hands the badge to him. Examining it under the glare of his desk lamp, Cornelius smiles his approval. He pulls hard on his cigarillo and then exhales. A veil of smoke crawls across his face, ascending to the noxious atmosphere hovering overhead. Ashes from his cigarillo drop onto the badge.

"That's it, Borj?" quizzes Cornelius.

He coughs violently, bending over double like he's trying to cough up a dead cat. He gasps for breath. His face turns red.

"Ya okay?"

"Yeah, I'm fine. Borj a first or last name?"

"Both."

"Borj Borj? Sounds strange."

"Just Borj."

On the request form, Cornelius writes 'Just' in the field for the applicant's first name. Borj makes no attempt to correct him, having tired of the mind-numbing process. Ashes from the cigarillo drift onto the form. Cornelius makes no attempt to brush them away. He switches on the laminating machine.

"This'll take a minute. Machine has to warm up," he explains, trying unsuccessfully to suppress a coughing-up-a-lung cough. His face turns deep red and then purplish red. He fights for air.

A frown crosses Borj's face. "Ya sure you're okay?"

Cornelius nods yes, unable to speak. Between coughing fits, he laminates the badge and affixes it to a lanyard. Occasionally, he wipes spittle from his mouth, using his dun-stained sleeve as a hankie. He drops the badge-replacement form on the counter.

"Sign here," he coughs, pointing at the bottom of the form.

Borj maneuvers the bottom of the paper within reach of the pen and scribbles a hasty signature.

"Ya should see a doctor. That's a bad cough."

Shaking his head, Cornelius stops coughing and gasps a deep breath. He grins. Leaning forward over his desk, he extends the badge to Borj, who reaches to take it. The wily codger playfully jerks it away just out of Borj's reach.

"Ya sure ya want it?" he demands playfully.

Exasperated, Borj lunges forward and snatches it.

"I'm joking with ya. Can't ya take a joke? She's all yours, a frigging work of art. You'll get the permanent replacement in the mail. If ya don't get it in two weeks, come and see me. Likely it got lost. That happens; ya can't trust the government for nothing, not even delivering the mail. Try not to lose it. Getting a temp for a temp is next to impossible. Best I can do at that point is give ya a whole new name," he adds, stifling a chuckle, so as not to induce another coughing fit. "Return this badge to me when ya get the new one."

"Thanks."

"No problem. Glad to help. Another satisfied customer," he adds with a knowing smile and a wink. "See ya around, kid." He slides shut the glass panel, plants himself on his chair, props his feet on his desk, picks up his newspaper and resumes reading.

With the rank odor of Cornelius' cigarillo clinging to him, Borj approaches the security guards. He proudly waves his badge, as if waving the national flag.

Barr reaches out and stops Borj, who is about to open the door.

"Now what?"

"Let's have a look," says Barr, inspecting Cornelius' handiwork. "The fossil did a good job. Now you're ID'd. Put it on, will ya?"

To appease Barr, Borj slips the lanyard over his head.

Barr smiles his security smile.

Borj opens the door and enters the office.

The closing door creates a whoosh of air.

'Ffft,' hermetically proclaims the rubberized door seal.

'Click,' says the door latch.

A vault-like silence prevails.

The Biz

Borj jams his time card into a punch clock. He checks his card and, satisfied, stuffs it in the 'In' rack. Taking a deep breath, he smears on a convincing smile and enters the waiting room.

The walls are covered with write-ups detailing the treachery of known super villains. Each write-up includes information about early childhood, descent into villainy, dirty tricks and deceptions, known associates, current whereabouts (if known), alleged crimes, criminal convictions, and so on. Some of the write-ups include a picture of the SV and others do not, depending on the SV's reclusiveness.

Two superheroes, Stapler-Man and Paper-Cut-Man, sit beside one another. Their costumes are clean and neatly pressed. A third superhero, Monk-Man, sitting in a corner facing a wall, wears a worn, black hoodie and faded blue jeans. Having pulled the hood over his head, he appears to be meditating. All of them are waiting for assignment.

"Hey," says Borj with a nod and a smile at Stapes and P-Cut.

Smiling coolly, Stapes raises his hand in the profile of a handgun and gives it a quick, ninety-degrees twist back and forth. He is thinking of trade-marking his signature wave to help advance his brand recognition on the national stage. A superhero knows he or she has triumphed when chosen to wear the logo of a corporation with a countrywide presence. Acquiring such an endorsement is unlikely, given his current T3 designation. Stapes needs at least a T2 standing. The task is daunting, but he is prepared to do whatever it takes. At present, Stapes wears on his cape the symbol of local scrap yard, Scrapper World. The emblem is the size of a bread-and-butter plate.

To advance his ambition, Stapes has hired a marketing agency, Big I Co. Stapes refers to Big I Co. and the agency's representative, RexlesWhind, as Stapes' Posse. Rex fields potential advertising requests from businesses, and schedules appearances at trade shows. With a T3 standing, there are few takers. 'Many aspire, but few are chosen.' Rex is fond of saying. Stapes has high hopes and is prepared to do his heroic best.

P-Cut is too engrossed in his current origami project to acknowledge Borj's presence. He's constructing a likeness of an SV. P-Cut's origami helps him pass the time while waiting for a mission. He has copyrighted several well-known and lesser known superhero and super-villain origami pieces and is working with a toy company, Kids in a Box Co., to develop an origami kit for children. The company wants to launch the product in time for fiscal quarter Q3, the Christmas season, with personal appearances by P-Cut, who will demonstrate how easy it is to construct heroes and villains. All you do is follow the instructions printed on each sheet of paper provided in the kit. Part of the challenge is to take P-Cut's complex origami pieces and simplify them for the target audience, kids ten and older. There are also legal concerns about creating likenesses of superheroes and villains. Contract talks between P-Cut and Kids in a Box Co. are progressing.

Borj nods at Lydia, the Assistant Office Manager, who is at her desk where she guards the door to the manager's office. 'Clayton Pitts' says a sign on the door to the inner sanctum. She returns a perfunctory business smile, glances at a clock and makes a mental note of the time.

Something's up, Borj concludes. *Better be on my best behavior.*

Electing to make a show of interest, he pulls a pair of reading glasses from his cape and slips them on. He peruses the super villain write-ups, stopping in front of the one for Fear-Monger-Man. As the political leader for the Grow a Pair Party, Fear-Monger-Man exploits the weaknesses of others. His specialty is preying on the ignorance and fears of the public. He spews his ham-fisted demagoguery to incite a culture of fear. He is often seen in the company of Bellicose-Man, Accusation-Man, and a cadre of lesser minions (for example, Pander-Man), who aid Fear-Monger-Man to curry favor. Fear-Monger-Man leaves a trail of destruction in his wake. Burdened with an overwhelming sense of terror and confusion, his victims, in their desperate desire to resolve the dilemma fashioned by Fear-Monger-Man, see only two equally unrealistic options: shit or go blind. When all seems lost, Fear-Monger-Man steps in, offering his victims, who have become his followers, a horrific solution that supports his dark ends. If left unchecked, Fear-Monger-Man will seek a position of unquestioned authority on the world stage.

"Good to know," Borj mutters loudly enough for Lydia to hear. Satisfied that his demonstration of interest has had the desired effect, he grabs a magazine and takes a seat.

"Important to stay current," says Borj holding up a well-thumbed copy of the publication *Super Villains*.

On the cover is the title for the lead article, 'Drummer-Boy – Friend or Foe?' Drummer-Boy is the CEO of a pan-denominational not-for-profit company that believes in the physical return of its once and future king, who will herald a global epoch of sweetness and light. Drummer-Boy seeks to drum up support for his belief by conveying a sense of innocence, hence the name Drummer-Boy. Members of his flock who stray from the true path are considered a threat to his organization, DB Inc. Accused of heresy, apostates are tried at a pseudo drumhead court-martial, stripped of their worldly possessions and banished from the flock. Justice is swift.

Borj opens the magazine to the main article.

"Hey," whispers Stapes, nudging P-Cut.

P-Cut ignores him.

"Hey," repeats Stapes, nudging him a little harder.

"What?" says P-Cut irritably. "I'm trying to concentrate."

"Check it out," he whispers with a smirk and a glance at Borj's boots. In addition to the numerous knotted repairs to the laces, the boots look like they were mauled by a belt sander.

P-Cut smiles scornfully and shakes his head at what he sees. "We have standards," he mutters, returning to his origami.

"Hey, Borj," says Stapes.

Borj looks up from his magazine.

"What happened to your boots? Attacked by a lawnmower?"

P-Cut chuckles while trying to maintain his concentration. "I'm trying to work here. Don't get me started. Villains are tough. Getting the mouth right on Sophistry-Man isn't easy."

Borj frowns, looking annoyed. He resumes reading, having decided not to escalate the issue.

Lydia picks up the phone on her desk. "He's here," she says quietly. "He came in about ten minutes ago. Yes, okay." She hangs up.

"Nice ID badge," comments Stapes, looking to pass the time. "Where did ya get it?"

"Cornelius," answers Borj without looking up from his magazine.

"Who?"

"The guy in the hallway, the one in the booth," says Borj looking up, unable to concentrate on the magazine article.

"Oh him. I hear ya had a run in with Hyperbole-Man last week," continues Stapes. "They interviewed him on

TV. He claimed he blew ya away. Said he used your cape to blow his nose. Looks like it too."

"Ya know how SVs are," says Borj defensively. "Consider the source. Talk is cheap."

"Yeah yeah. That's not how I heard it. I heard he used ya like a toilet brush cleaning up turds at the Millhouse sewage plant."

Before Borj can reply, Monk begins to shake. He stops, having managed to control himself. Then he starts shaking again. His trembling becomes progressively worse. His chair, shuddering violently, slowly slides across the floor before coming to a halt about mid-floor. Monk, looking unsteady, picks up his chair and returns to his corner.

"Is it me, or is the room getting warmer?" Borj asks, looking concerned. "Is he okay? Hey Monk, ya okay?"

There's no response from Monk.

Lydia frowns. "Isn't anyone going to help?"

"Ah, ya know how these guys are," Stapes answers.

"What, Post Traumatic Stress Syndrome?"

"More like PDVS," answers P-Cut, without looking up from his work.

"PDVS?" asks Borj.

"Post Dramatic Villain Syndrome," responds P-Cut. "They're drama queens."

Borj goes to the water cooler and fills a paper cup.

"Here, try this," he says, offering the cup to Monk. There's no response. His face is hidden by his hood. Borj sets the cup down beside Monk and returns to his seat.

"What's up with him?" queries Borj, looking at Stapes and P-Cut.

"Former SV turned good. It happens," answers Stapes. "He used to be Hothead-Man."

"Yeah," chimes in P-Cut, "tried to give everyone in the city a hot head. He wanted to make them start arguing and fighting. Best he could do was give hot heads to little kids; made them faint."

"Puppies too," adds Stapes, grinning from ear to ear. "He was pathetic. Ya should've seen the mothers of those little kids beat the snot out of him. Isn't that right Monk?"

Monk is silent on the matter.

"No wonder he gave up on villainy" responds P-Cut. "And ya can't trust him. He's like the rest of them. They always want to go back. They don't usually last long here before falling back on their old ways."

"Once an SV, always an SV," Stapes adds. "And get this; right now, he's learning all our trade secrets."

"They learn our weaknesses and our strengths," P-Cut validates, "and then they use them against us next time we run into them."

"Yeah yeah. They come out of here knowing more about us than we do. They know how we think and our every superhero move," Stapes corroborates. Stapes is getting hot under the cape over the sense of injustice unwittingly perpetrated by the very agency that should be looking after his welfare. "And what does NPA do? Nothing, absolutely nothing. It's not NPA management that has to go out and face these guys once an SV goes rogue again."

"Keep it down," Borj cautions. "He can hear ya."

"So what?" says P-Cut, raising his voice. "It's only a matter of time before he goes back to where he came from. Isn't that right Monk, or should I say Hothead-Man?"

"Knock it off. At least he's trying," says Borj, beginning to get heated too.

"Look. Monk's got ya all worked up," Stapes observes.

"It's not Monk! It's this conversation," retorts the frustrated Borj. "We're doing this to ourselves. It has nothing to do with Monk."

"I hope it's you that has to deal with him next time," grouses Stapes. "Matter of fact, I'll insist on it."

Lydia's phone rings. "Okay, I'll tell him," she answers. "Borj, Clay wants to see you now."

Forget That

"Hi Clay," says Borj, entering Clay's office. "Ya wanted to see me?"

Parked behind his desk, Clay, with his back to Borj, stares at the plethora of charts and graphs plastered on the wall.

"Come in," says Clay, turning his graying, crew-cut head to glance at Borj. He does a double-take, looking askance through his fish-eyed glasses at Borj's dilapidated appearance. "Close the door and have a seat." He swivels his pear-shaped body to align it with his head. "I've been meaning to talk to you. How long has it been since we last talked, six months?"

"About a year."

"How long have you been in the superhero business?"

"Almost eleven years."

"You know most superheroes move on after about ten years. It's a tough life. Ever thought of a career change? It might do you good. You wouldn't be the first. Look at E-Reader-Man. He used to spin tales around SVs until they didn't know if they were coming or going. He was smooth. He's writing his memoirs now. Has an agent and a book deal. You might want to think about it. It's a suggestion."

"I know it sounds weird, but I have this feeling. There's something not finished, or maybe not started. Like I'm waiting, but I don't know what it is I'm waiting for." Borj struggles to put into words what is little more than a premonition. "Do ya ever get a feeling that won't go away, like a song stuck in your head? The feeling that there's something ya need to do or say. And ya have to make it happen in the right way. Ya can't bulldoze your way through to get the result ya want the way we do here. It's not about playing soccer with an SV's nut sack and then calling it a day." He looks intently at Clay, hoping that his explanation is seeping in beyond the wall of charts and graphs. "Is any of this making sense?"

"You mean destiny?" queries the floundering Clay.

"It's not that. It's not like it's written in stone. It's more like an opportunity to make a choice and making the right one isn't a certainty. Or maybe it's a bunch of choices that strung together are important. Somehow, I have to try, or be ground down to nothing."

A spell has been cast. Silence fills the room. Clay stares blankly at Borj. He clears his throat, hoping to recover his focus. He is unsuccessful.

"Why am I here? Is that what you mean?"

"Yeah, why?"

Clay shakes his head in disbelief, breaking the spell. "Forget that. You don't have time. Focus. Listen to what I'm going to tell you. It's time to get down to business." He looks at a graph and points vaguely at it for Borj's edification. "You know what this is?"

"It's a pie chart."

"Yes, that's right. And this one?" asks Clay, pointing to another piece of paper.

"Bar chart," responds Borj with a look of resignation.

Irritated, Clay scowls, as though schooling a lapsed novice. "I'm doing this for your benefit."

"My bad," Borj confesses.

Satisfied with Borj's contrition, Clay continues. "Work with me on this. Do you know what they tell me?"

Borj shrugs, although he knows the answer.

"They tell me things aren't going well," states Clay. "See this bar? This is you. And this one is Stapler-Man and this is Paper-Cut-Man. These other bars represent the rest of the crew that work out of this office. Notice anything about yours?"

"Mine's a little longer."

"Yours is much longer. Do you know what that means?"

"Nothing good, I'm sure, if we're having this conversation."

"This is the DDWEwtE bar graph, Damage Done While Engaged with the Enemy; DDWE for short. It tells me that after you engage an SV, this is the amount of collateral damage done to property while you're defeating the SV. You're off the chart. We're talking millions of dollars. And this pie chart shows the amount of time it takes a superhero to subdue an SV. This slice is you. It's huge compared to the others. What gives? I've got a meeting downtown tomorrow with my director. I need answers. What am I going to tell him about your performance?"

"Dyspepsia-Man wasn't easy. I had heartburn for a week after. Then there was Enabler-Man who had everybody in the neighborhood engaged in one scheme or another and to what end I don't know. I couldn't tell who was working for who."

"You mean who was working for whom," Clay corrects.

"Defeating him and the enabled horde was like trying to herd wolverines. And cutting through the bullshit of Hyperbole-Man and his sidekick, Truth-Bender-Boy, took time. It seemed like almost everyone in Lore was on their side. And don't forget Prevaricator-Woman. Listening to her made me dizzy. She said stuff that almost made sense. She talked about the one who is coming. I didn't..."

"Not good enough," says Clay, cutting off Borj. "Look at the stats on Paper-Cut-Man. He would have finished off Prevaricator-Woman with a dozen or so paper cuts. You listen to these SVs too much. Stop it. They're inhuman. They're targets to be eliminated. I want no more excuses.

What's your designation here anyway?" Clay asks, knowing the answer.

"T3, like everyone else here."

"No, what's your sub-category?"

"J"

"T3-J, tier-three superhero, junior class. You used to be a tier two, senior. You were on your way up. You were headed for the big leagues, tier one. Now you can't even handle T3 SVs, and some of them hardly qualify for a T3 classification. They're more like T4. You should be able to finish them off in no time at all."

"Ya know the city skews the SV ratings. They deliberately downgrade an SV to save money. It's a lot less expensive to send a T3 superhero against a SV than it is to send a T2 or T1. And the SV with the bogus ranking feels obligated to prove that he's better than the one fabricated by the city. That leads to more collateral damage. Then the city complains about the damage when it takes longer to finish off an SV. Ya get what ya pay for."

"What happened to you? You were good. You didn't make excuses. You got the job done. You're becoming a liability."

"I hesitated. I had him and I choked."

"Had who? What are you talking about?"

"Victim-Man, ya know the guy. He's always protesting that he's the injured party, not the perpetrator. He blames the real victims, or anyone who comes to their aid. It's part of his MO."

"That loser!" retorts Clay. "You let that little weasel get the better of you? What were you thinking?"

"For a second I saw him as he really is, his weakness. I don't mean weakness in the sense of a vulnerability to be exploited. It was a revelation. I hesitated. Then my training kicked in and I blew him away."

"That's better. That's what I like to hear. That note you produce with your sax can blow away almost anyone."

"Since Victim-Man... I don't know."

40

"You don't know?" Clay asks rhetorically. "Look, your sax is your saving grace. Keep that focus. You hang back again the way you did with Victim-Man, you'll be looking for a new job. Hesitating leads to more collateral damage. The stats prove it. You can't afford to dither and this agency can't afford it either. When the mayor calls on us for help, he expects results. And if he isn't happy with the results, I'm not happy. We're running a service here. And there are lots of franchise operations like ours that would be happy to get Lore's business. If you screw up and the city calls on us less often, that means less revenue for this agency. The income generated per superhero declines and that stat is one of the key measures for my annual bonus. I'm forced to look for ways to improve the stat when it drops. That means letting one of the underperforming superheroes go."

"If ya could have seen him," says Borj, pleading for a little understanding. "For a moment, I saw his weakness in myself."

"He was manipulating you. And besides, we're not social workers. We're not here to provide a come-to-Jesus moment for these SVs. They're vile and despicable. No more of this bleeding-heart stuff. I don't want to hear it. They don't deserve it. They deserve to be locked up in The Millhouse. If you don't stop making bad choices, it's going to cost you."

"He could've been any one of us! You'd know that, if ya had to deal with one of them."

"I've got overhead. There's this office, Lydia, security, you and the other T3s. I have people that I answer to. Their only interests are the stats and the bottom line," retorts Clay, having run out of patience. "Senior management is talking about bringing in T3s from other countries at a cheaper rate. That means you and others, like Stapler-Man and Paper-Cut-Man, could be out of jobs. I'm not saying it's going to happen. I'm only saying you have to work harder and not pay attention to any feelings of," Clay hesitates while searching for the right word, "*sympathy* that you might have toward these SVs. Yes, that's it, sympathy," he adds, feeling pleased with himself. "Look after number one. That's you. No one else will. Stay positive. Be resilient. Accept responsibility for your mistakes. For God's sake do the right thing!" He pauses, thinking about what he has to say next. "Look, I have no choice. I'm putting you on probation. Another slip up like Victim-Man and you'll be out of a job. That's final."

"What about a transfer to a T4 unit? Maybe I could be a T4 superhero."

"I checked. No T4 unit will have you. And you'd be at the bottom with a T4 ranking. You'd be down to scraping gum off sidewalks after nuisance SVs like Bubble-Gum-Guy. I've seen it before, guys like you who show promise. You're on your way up, headed for the major leagues, and then… I don't know. You screw up and it's a downhill slide. If I was a betting man, I'd give you about a week before you packed it in as a T4. You don't want to go there."

"Okay," says Borj, staggered by the turn of events. He decides this isn't a good time to ask for an advance on his salary.

"Remember. Stay focused. Stay tough. This is your last chance. I'm sticking my neck out for you. No more slip ups. This is a business, not a charity. I can't keep carrying you like this."

Borj returns to the waiting room. Discouraged, he slumps onto a chair.

Lydia smiles sympathetically.

Morning meanders into afternoon.

Borj mulls over his meeting with Clay. He tries to read magazines and study SV write-ups. He can't concentrate. P-Cut spends time developing his origami characters. Stapes practices his quick draw with his latest matched set of staplers that he designed himself. He calls his latest model The Decider.

A Mission

"Okay," yells Clay, bursting out of his office, "we've got a live one. Guy named Disposal-Man. Who wants it?"

The superheroes look at the clock. It's almost five-thirty, quitting time.

"Can't the after-core-hours team handle this?" P-Cut asks.

"No!" answers Clay. "I need someone now. We're short of our quota this month. I need an SV encounter on the books from one of you. Who's it going to be?"

"Why is this coming in so late?" asks Stapes.

"There was a communication foul up at the central office."

"Where's the call?" queries Borj.

"Northwest end of the city in the Middleman suburb. Who's taking this? I need an answer."

"That's way out in the middle of nowhere," Borj grumbles. "Take at least an hour to get out there by subway. It's the end of the line. Transits stops running at midnight. Ya could get stranded out there with no way back until morning. Ya willing to spring for cab fare?"

"No, you're on your own, no cab fare. This franchise can't afford it. You know that as well as I do."

"Well that sucks," carps Stapes.

"Who's taking this?"

"Huddle up boys," instructs Borj.

P-Cut and Stapes huddle with Borj. Monk's status as an apprentice denies him a say in the outcome.

"One of us needs to take it. How do we decide this?"

"The way we always do," says P-Cut, winking at Stapes.

"That's right," says Stapes with a knowing nod at his accomplice. "I'll call it. Ya ready? First guy out accepts the mission. Here we go, rock, paper, scissors," he chants with their hands pumping in unison.

"Nuts!" mutters Borj. "I always get the short end." He looks suspiciously at his grinning cohorts. "Next time we'll use a different game."

"Yeah yeah. Sure thing," Stapes responds.

"Borj's on it," yells P-Cut.

"Good," says Clay, relieved that there's a decision. "Take Hothead, I mean Monk-Man with you. Show him the ropes."

"Come on Monk. Let's go."

"Wait," orders Clay. "Where's your sax?"

"I pawned it."

"You did what? Unbelievable! What are you going to do, bore this guy to death with stories of your past glory? Stapler-Man, give Borj one of your staplers. Paper-Cut-Man, give him some of your paper supply. Maybe ya can use them."

"All right, ya can have an old staple gun. It's an early prototype. And this is the first and last time," warns Stapes. "I'm not carrying ya. Bring your own tools next time. Wait here. I'll get it."

"I've got some old Lickspittle newspapers," P-Cut offers grudgingly. "They're wet. Ya can have them. After this, that's it, no more. I'm not going to carry ya either. Hothead-Man can cart them. He can use my old wheelbarrow."

Stapes returns lugging a suitcase with both hands. The suitcase is the size of a bar fridge. He sets down the case beside Borj.

"It's heavy. Don't worry. It can stop an elephant at a hundred yards," says Stapes. "I threw in a couple of ammo clips. The staples are specially made, titanium. Don't go wasting ammunition. It's expensive stuff. I expect ya to pay me for any ya use. Ya should do a test fire to get the hang of it. It's got a kick. Make sure ya take your time. You'll be okay. Be careful; it doesn't have a safety. That ought to do it," says Stapes, feeling pleased with himself.

Borj hasn't time to ask questions before P-Cut returns with a wheelbarrow stacked high with bundles of newspapers.

"It's tippy. Watch yourself," cautions P-Cut. "I'm not going to let ya have my truck. I can't afford having some amateur wreck it. You can make do with the wheelbarrow."

Borj looks in disbelief at the stack of musty paper.

"Monk, ya ready?" Borj wonders what he's got himself into. There's no answer from Monk. "Hey Monk, come on. Let's go. Grab the wheelbarrow." Seizing the case, he makes a mental note that somehow, he must get his sax out of hawk.

Monk stirs.

"Here," says Clay, thrusting a sheet of paper at Monk. "It's the write-up for Disposal-Man. It isn't much. Study it on the way. You can take the maintenance elevator at the subway station."

Monk stuffs the paper into the muff of his hoodie. He grabs the wheelbarrow, heaves it up and lumbers off behind Borj.

Getting There

Borj argues with the authorities at the Drifton station. There is a heated exchange about the fare. He contends they are performing a public service and should not be required to pay. In the end Borj relents. Monk seems oblivious to the idea of commerce, making Borj wonder how Monk survived in the role of an SV, or an ordinary citizen for that matter. They take the maintenance elevator to the train platform where they wait for the next outbound train to Middleman.

A rush of air precedes the incoming train.

"Get ready," says Borj. "We'll need to work fast."

The train stops. The doors open. They rush toward an open door. Monk propels the wheelbarrow into the subway car. A few of the newspaper bundles fall off, flopping like wet rags onto the platform floor. Grabbing the disintegrating bundles, they manhandle them onto the train, leaving some soggy remnants stranded.

"Forget the rest!" Borj orders. "There isn't time."

The doors slide shut. The train accelerates. Panting hard from their exertions, they sit down.

"When we get there, follow my lead," Borj insists, flashing a two-fingered, watch-me gesture. "Are ya listening?"

There's no response from Monk, who seems preoccupied with the other commuters.

"Hey! Stop that!" Borj demands, noticing Monk's roving eye. "Leave them alone. Stay focused. Eyes on me! We've got a job to do."

"My bad," acknowledges Monk, embarrassed by his mistake. "Old habits die hard. It won't happen again."

The train rumbles down the track, swaying from side to side. Borj keeps a wary eye on Monk and the precarious stack of newspapers.

"What's the NPA scandal sheet say about Disposal-Man?"

Monk pulls out the crumpled sheet of paper.

"Not much here. This is a preliminary report from Intelligence. Looks like it was done in a hurry. Origin of Disposal-Man unknown and there's no biography. He's made of a metal alloy, a mechanical robot by the sounds of this description: roughly eight-feet tall and weighing about a quarter ton. It's a best guess. Very agile. Observed eating metal objects, mostly cars and trucks."

"That must be why they call him Disposal-Man."

"According to this he's got some sort of mark, like a tattoo, on the back of his head. Looks like a garbage can. It could be a symbol representing his designation, or maybe the equivalent of a bar code. Linguistics at Intel says it could mean 'disposal'. Sex is indeterminate. Subject to change, they named it Disposal-Man. Report goes on to say that he devours vehicles like he's at an all-you-can-eat buffet. That might explain the neighborhood, mostly middle class with lots of vehicles. Must be incredibly strong. He has an aversion to wood products."

"Wood products?"

"Yeah trees, that kind of thing."

"Ya must have some insight into SVs. What's this guy like?"

"He's probably like the rest of us, insecure, afraid, looking for that one thing that's going to take away his fears. Until he finds an answer to his dilemma, he's feeding the beast. And the beast is never satisfied."

"That's it? That's the best ya can do? Haven't ya got anything concrete that I can work with. My collateral damage number is way off the chart. If I don't bring it down, I'll be out of a job. Ya got anything else on this guy?"

"We're no different than you."

"You're not helping. What am I supposed to do with that? What's this guy's weak spot, his Achilles heel? And what's this *we* stuff? You're on our side now. I can't afford to have you going off the rails."

"Let's try it another way," replies Monk, struggling to remain placid. "Who are you?"

"What! What is this, some sort of self-analysis?" asks Borj in disbelief. "I don't have time for this. I need a quick-fix, not navel gazing. Who's the apprentice here?"

"The truth is here," responds Monk, surveying his surroundings.

"Ah crap! My head hurts. It must be the moldy papers. Does this car seem stuffy? Hey!" exclaims Borj, seizing on a new idea. "What are ya trying to pull?"

"Who's driving the train?" Monk answers.

"Great! I've got some newspapers, an oversized staple gun and a guy who talks in riddles. And somehow, I'm supposed to take down a metal monster with an aversion to wood. What am I going to do, trap him in a wooden crate? What next?"

"We're here," observes Monk, as the train pulls into the last station in the line.

"Where?"

"The station. You should try to be more aware of your surroundings."

"What?" Borj looks out a window as the train glides to a stop. "Here already?"

Borj and Monk wait patiently beside a deserted bus stop, having hauled their doubtful weaponry up a flight of stairs from the subway platform below.

"I need an update," says Borj, out of breath after the physical exertion. "There's a phone over there. I'll see if Intel can tell us anything new. I'll be back in a minute. Don't move." He hustles over to a nearby payphone.

"Yeah, it's me," says Borj. "What ya got for me? What do ya mean, who is this? It's me, Borj. Who do ya think it is? What's the latest intelligence on this Disposal-Man guy? Where is he? The parking lot of the Middlemass Haven Plaza? Where's that in relationship to the…" Borj glances around looking for a name of the subway station. "Gristmill. Ah shit!" Monk has deserted the stapler and newspapers. He is nowhere to be seen. "Crap! I've lost Monk. He's gone, disappeared. How do I know where he went? Just tell me where the plaza is. Where? That's on the other side of Middleman. Can ya send transport? No, well ya got any new info on this Disposal guy? His boots aren't made of metal. What're they made of? Ya think it's some sort of synthetic rubber product. Ya mean like tires? That's it? That's all ya got for me? Someone's sniffing around the staple gun. I've got to go before he steals it. If Monk calls in, tell him to get his ass back here." He slams down the receiver.

"Hey! Get away from that!" yells Borj, running back to the bus stop.

Borj waits anxiously for a bus, uncertain how he will manage both the stapler and the newspapers. A line of passengers has formed behind him. A bus pulls up and the doors open. Borj grabs the stapler case.

"Whoa!" says the bus driver, sounding frazzled after a long shift. "Ya can bring the case on, but not the newspapers. This isn't a truck."

Borj stops in mid-step.

"Hi, Debbie," responds Borj, looking at the name sewn on the bus driver's blouse. "This is an emergency. I have to get to the Middlemass Haven Plaza. There's a metal…"

"I have a schedule to keep," says Debbie, cutting off Borj. "Please step aside, Sir, and let the other passengers board. Next time, plan ahead. If ya have papers that need recycling, find a better way to get them to the recycle depot. Now, please step aside and let the others on."

"Look, it's very important…"

Borj is interrupted by someone tapping on his shoulder.

"Hang on a minute!" says Borj, turning to address whoever is trying to get his attention. "Will ya please …" Borj stops in mid-sentence.

"I've got wheels," says Monk. "Grab your stuff. Let's go."

Following Monk, Borj is astounded by what he finds behind the bus.

"What's this?" asks Borj.

"Our ride." Monk answers, smiling triumphantly at a small, rundown farm tractor. Behind it is an equally dilapidated wagon with bulbous tires and corrugated, sheet-metal siding.

"Where did ya get this?"

"Don't ask. We're parked in a bus loading zone. We've got to get out of here. Where are we going?"

"Middlemass Haven Plaza," answers Borj, heaving bundles of newspapers into the wagon. "Ya know where it is?"

"I know it," says Monk, throwing on the last bundle. "I'll drive. Get on."

Borj grabs the stapler case and jumps on the wagon.

What's the Plan?

After a bone-rattling ride, Monk circles the plaza looking for Disposal-Man.

"That's him," shouts Monk, pulling into the parking lot.

Having already consumed a dozen or so vehicles, Disposal-Man tears off the hood of a pickup truck and bites off a piece, as though eating a lettuce leaf. He ignores their arrival.

"Pull up over there," yells Borj.

Monk stops a safe distance from Disposal-Man. With the engine still running, Monk scoots behind the wagon where Borj has established an observation post.

"I left the tractor running. If I turn it off, it might not restart. What's the plan?"

"Don't know. Let's watch and see what he does."

Having finished the hood, Disposal-Man rips out the engine, bites off a piece, chews, spits out the non-metallic bits, and swallows.

Borj quietly opens the stapler case. He pulls out the size-of-a-timber-wolf stapler, grabs a clip of staples and, after a little fumbling, slams it home.

"Stay here," Borj whispers. "I want to get a closer look."

"What do you want me to do?"

"Watch. See what he does. Don't try anything," Borj cautions.

Monk nods.

Crouched low and with stapler in hand, Borj lumbers off, shielding himself behind a row of vehicles. He stops short of his target and peers over a car.

The monster is human in shape with a torso and limbs in the style of a rat bike cobbled together from a jumble of components of various shapes and sizes. The overall impression is that of an inuksuk. Body parts are charred charcoal black. Scarcely visible on many body parts are strange symbols, possibly maintenance instructions. The head is anchored to a massive pair of shoulders. The arms end in hands the size of microwave ovens. The legs are the size of tree trunks, and the enormous feet evenly distribute the being's weight.

Borj looks down the row of vehicles to the place where he left Monk. There's no sign of him.

"Shit, where's he gone this time?" he complains. Anxiously, Borj scans for the apprentice. He catches sight of him standing in the parking lot, clearly exposed to the beast.

"No! What's he done?" mutters Borj.

Too late to stop him, Borj turns his attention once more to Disposal-Man.

Monk, having pried up a manhole cover, has sent it rolling on its wobbly way toward the alien. The cover slowly picks up speed on the gentle downward slope, achieving the modest velocity of a human out for a leisurely stroll.

Borj raises the stapler. "This is it." He places an uneasy finger on the trigger.

Monk's projectile nudges Disposal-Man on the heel.

The machine twists round with the speed and agility of a leopard. The cover stops and twirls round and round in a death spiral. Disposal-Man watches. Faster and faster the cover spins, sinking lower and lower. With a final shudder, the cover stops. The titan reaches down and picks it up. He looks at it for a moment.

"Here we go," murmurs Borj. He aims the stapler. His trigger finger twitches.

Disposal-Man bites into the cover the way you would an oatmeal raisin cookie.

'Kffpp,' says the stapler.

Borj has accidentally squeezed off a round. The staple misses the beast, instead imbedding itself in the engine block of a nearby truck.

Disposal-Man, who is busy finishing the manhole cover, seems not to have noticed.

"Hi Borj," says a cheerful voice beside him.

"What are ya doing here? This is no place for you! Get down!" Borj orders, glancing at his sister, Joki. He makes a grab for her arm to pull her down, behind the safety of the car.

She's too quick for him, taking a step back out of his reach.

"Where did you come from?"

"Well, nice to see you too. Didn't you see me walking across the parking lot? I waved at you. Why don't you pay more attention to what's going on? And don't be so grabby!"

"Will ya please get down," pleads Borj.

"I saw you and your friend when you turned into the parking lot. I thought I'd come over and see how things are going," she answers casually, while brushing a wrinkle from her pants. She makes no effort to hide. "I haven't seen you in a while. What've you been up to? And what are you doing down there? Stand up. You're a mess. Take some pride in your appearance." She bends over and sniffs Borj's attire. Repulsed, she straightens up. "Phew! What's that smell? You smell musty? What are you up to? And what's with the tractor?"

"I haven't time to explain. Ya shouldn't be here! It's too dangerous! At least get down so he can't see ya."

"So who can't see me?"

"Hello! See the big, metal can opener over there eating that truck?" whispers the agitated Borj from his crouched position.

Disposal-Man peels off roof of the vehicle, rolls it into a cylinder and eats it like a celery stick. He looks in the direction of the diminutive Joki. He pauses, evaluating her as a potential threat.

"Oh him," she retorts. "Are you going to let *that* intimidate you?" she challenges.

Striking a defiant stance, Joki confronts the fiend. She looks like a torch with her swept-back reddish orange hair and raven-black jacket and pants. She waves a dismissive hand at Disposal-Man in response to the unwanted attention. A bracelet jangles and disappears up the sleeve of her porcelain-white blouse.

"Shoo!" she commands with a feisty glare, as though putting the run to a stray cat.

There's no response from the colossus.

"Get lost!" she orders, taking a step toward the giant.

The situation is escalating.

Seeing his chance, Borj grabs her hand and tugs, attempting to pull her down behind the safety of the car.

"Stop that!" Joki demands, remaining steadfast. She shakes free and glowers at the metal adversary, who refuses to obey.

"Hey you, metal head! I'm warning you. Don't make me come over there!" she threatens, ramping up the rhetoric as one might when confronting a school bully.

Unperturbed, the goliath tears off the tailgate and resumes his meal.

"What's his problem?" she asks, flabbergasted by the alien's indifference. "And where's your sax? You didn't leave it in your apartment again, did you? How do you expect to get anything done without it?" she demands. "Honestly, focus, will you?"

"It's a long story. I haven't time to explain. Right now, my job is to stop that thing before it eats every vehicle in the place."

"What do you have in the way of resources?"

"I've got a loose cannon called Monk-Man. He used to be a super villain. He wasn't very good. His claim to fame was making little kids sick. Their mothers beat the crap out of him when they realized what he was up to."

"Okay, that's a start," Joki encourages. "What else?"

"I've got this staple gun that can stop a train and I've got a wagon-load of soggy newspapers."

"Okay, you're good to go then. You can do this," Joki responds confidently.

"What are ya talking about? If ya have some ideas, let's hear them."

"You lure him to The Flour Mill. That gets him away from the people and cars. Once you get him there, you trap him. What could be simpler? I'm done here. I'll see you later."

"Wait! Fill in some of the blanks, will ya? How do I get him over there? Trap him how? I need details."

"Oh details! You've got lots of paper, haven't you?"

"Yeah, what do ya want me to do? Corner him and read him to death with the Lickspittle? I'm not E-Reader-Man!"

"Must I explain everything? I've got to go. I'm late. I'll leave the rest to you."

"Wait!"

The sound of metal being ripped apart rents the air.

Borj glances at Disposal-Man, who is busy tearing apart the truck frame and stuffing the pretzel-like pieces into his maw.

"Who are you talking to?" asks Monk, hunkering down beside the preoccupied Borj.

"My sister."

"Where? I don't see her."

"She was here a minute ago."

"Next time introduce me, will you? What does she look like?"

"Never mind. We've got work to do. Stay focused. And what was that stunt with the manhole cover?"

"I wanted to see his reaction. I've never seen a big guy move like that before. That was impressive."

"Okay, here's the plan. I'm going to take him down with this staple gun. Are ya ready?" Borj aims carefully at Disposal-Man.

"Wait! Let me…"

Borj fires off a round before Monk can finish his thought.

'Kffpp.'

'Tink,' says the staple, hitting Disposal-Man. The staple crumples harmlessly and falls to the ground.

Disposal-Man looks in Borj's direction.

"Crap!" curses Borj. "Let's get out of here!"

"No, wait a second. Let's watch," counters Monk.

Disposal-Man reaches down, picks up the spent staple, inspects it and then eats it.

"Hey, I think he likes it," observes Monk. "Fire off another one."

'Kffpp.'

'Tink.'

Disposal-Man eats the second staple.

He tossed that back like it was popcorn," observes Borj. He fires a third staple with the same outcome.

"He really likes those." Monk responds, smiling.

The experiment quickly changes. Disposal-Man takes a step toward Borj and Monk.

"I guess this means we shouldn't feed the animals. Run!" orders Borj, who immediately takes off toward the tractor with Monk at his side.

Disposal-Man takes up pursuit.

"He doesn't run very fast! Let's see if we can get in front of this bad boy and keep his attention," Borj instructs.

"You drive. I'll get in the wagon and feed him staples. Head for The Flour Mill."

"Then what?"

"Don't know. Just do it!"

Borj throws the stapler and himself into the wagon.

The tractor lurches forward, moving marginally faster than Disposal-Man.

'Kffpp.'

'Tink.'

The behemoth stops, picks up the spent staple, ingests it and continues the sluggish chase.

Sweet Dreams

Monk navigates rush-hour traffic, sideswiping scores of vehicles in his frantic attempt to stay out of Disposal-Man's reach.

The tractor begins to overheat.

'Kffpp.' 'Tink.' 'Kffpp…' 'Tink…'

Monk reaches the parking lot of The Flour Mill. He's quickly running out of space. Smoke billows from the tractor engine. The giant is closing the gap. A red warning sign, 'Depleting', flashes on the stapler. The first clip is almost empty.

"Now where?" Monk yells. He coughs, trying to avoid the smoke while nervously glancing at Disposal-Man.

Borj fights off his rising panic. "Don't stop! Keep going! Go into the mill," hollers Borj, waving wildly at an open shipping door. "Over there! Go in there!"

He fires in quick succession his last two staples. Disposal-Man stops to eat them. Borj ejects the spent clip and jams in the remaining one.

Monk steers the tractor into the mill where the tractor quits in front of a row of old, concrete silos slated for demolition.

After a quick appraisal of his surroundings, Borj leaps out of the wagon. He swings open the steel doors to one of the silos. It's filled waist deep with flour. In the middle of the silo, a bunch of discarded, wooden pallets lie strewn on top of the flour.

"Here's what we're going to do," Borj explains. "I'm going in there. We know he wants the staples. After he follows me in, close and lock the doors."

"He'll kill you!" says Monk, glancing at the shipping doors. As yet, there is no sign of Disposal-Man.

"Ya have to slow him down. I need time."

"How?"

"See those sacks of flour up there on the catwalk," says Borj, pointing toward the top of the silo. "Dump them in the silo after ya lock us in. It'll give me some cover. But first, let's get the newspapers up there too."

"What do you want to do with the papers?" asks Monk, suppressing his rising anxiety.

"Throw them in with the flour. You'll see. Trust me on this." He smiles to hide his doubt. "I don't' have time to explain."

Borj punches a switch. A conveyor, running up the side of the silo, rumbles into action. They start throwing bundles of paper on the conveyor.

Borj looks Monk straight in the eye. "I'm counting on ya," hollers Borj over the clatter of the conveyor. "We can do this," he declares to bolster their confidence.

"I've got your back," answers Monk. He makes a thumbs-up gesture to reinforce his claim. "What're you going to do while I'm doing all this?"

"Trying not to get killed," says Borj, feeling uncertain about the outcome. He grins to relieve the tension. His smile is soon overshadowed by a silhouette that fills the shipping entrance.

"He's coming," shouts Borj, as he heaves the last of the papers onto the conveyor belt. "Hide somewhere, so he doesn't see ya."

Borj picks up the staple gun and heads into the silo. He wades through the flour. His progress is slow. With each step, he kicks up the powder, creating a cloud around him. His breathing is labored. Determined, he pushes on.

Clambering onto the pallets, Borj fires a volley of staples at the wall on the side opposite the doors, creating a ladder.

A shadow blocks the doorway to the silo.

Borj's heart is pounding. Gasping for breath and coughing, he leaps off the pallets and works his way to the far side of the silo. Frantically he scoops up the flour and throws it into the air, hoping to provide additional cover.

The machine squeezes through the door opening. He stands to his full height, towering above Borj.

"Now Monk, now!" Borj yells. There's no response. "Close the doors. Now!" hollers Borj. He's out of options.

The steel doors slam shut. Borj can hear heavy metal bars swinging closed. The machine bangs its fists, like wrecking balls, against the doors. The sound is deafening. Borj covers his ears. The doors refuse to budge.

Disposal-Man turns his attention to Borj, who chokes back a cough. The giant strides into the center of the silo, kicking up a mountain of flour. The wooden pallets crack under the weight of the behemoth.

Sensing an opportunity, Borj lurches forward and fires a torrent of staples. He beats a hasty retreat.

Disposal-Man lunges at Borj. His forward motion is impeded by an unseen force. The monster's boots are stapled to several pallets. The machine swings a massive hand, gouging deep grooves in the wall. Instinctively Borj ducks. Chunks of cement fly in all directions.

Angry and showing little sign of tiring, Disposal-Man rotates his entire body, overcoming the resistance of the pallets and flour. His arms act like the blades of a kitchen blender. The colossus spins faster, creating a vortex. The air grows thick with flour.

Borj can't stop coughing. He holds onto one of the staples in the silo wall. Terrified, he can feel the force of the whirlpool beginning to pull him toward the center. The staple begins to pull free. Borj looks toward the top of the silo. There is no sign of Monk. Nearing exhaustion, Borj has little left to give.

"Come on Monk!" he shouts. "Where are ya? I need ya now!"

From the top of the silo, Monk hurls sacks of flour at the leviathan. The whirling monster slashes open the falling sacks. The powder flies in all directions, smothering everything. Exhausting the flour supply, Monk launches the newspaper bundles, which are quickly shredded and blended with the flour.

"Okay," yells Monk, worn out by the effort. "It's all in! Borj, can you hear me?" There's no response from below, only the roar of the maelstrom. "Borj! Are you there?"

Holding tight, Borj aims the staple gun upward. He fires. Nothing happens. The red warning sign flashes; there are two staples left. Fighting to remain calm, he aims and fires again. Still nothing.

The staple he is holding onto rips free. He lurches upward and grabs the next rung in his staple ladder. Against the pull of the whirlpool and avoiding the deadly hands of Disposal-Man, Borj climbs. Barely able to hold on, he stops and fires skyward one last time. He drops the staple gun. It's of no further use to him. The creature's arms pulverize the gun into scrap metal.

Abruptly, water pours into the silo. Borj has hit an overhead water pipe. The concoction of flour, newspaper and water begins to thicken into papier-mâché that threatens to draw him downward. Desperately, he fights to pull himself up.

Disposal-Man grows heavier, owing to the clinging mixture that thoroughly coats his body. The added weight is rapidly draining his energy reserves. His spinning slows and finally stops. The leviathan clutches at a staple in the wall, frantic to pull himself from the quagmire. The rung gives way. He's too heavy. The gummy mess begins to set, slowly incarcerating him.

In one last desperate effort, the beast leaps at Borj, grabbing his cape. With a jolt, Borj stops his ascent and fights to hang on. The cloth rips along a perforation.

Disposal-Man sinks. His energy is nearly depleted. Fully immersed in the adhesive bog, he is suspended in his prison, frozen, as if in a pirouette.

Covered in the sticky substance, Borj drags himself up the remaining rungs to the top of the silo.

Monk pulls him out. He beams at Borj, relieved to see him.

"I'll turn off the water," says Borj. "Use your heat and bake that mess. Make it rock solid."

"I can't. I took an oath not to use it," protests Monk.

"Ya don't have a choice. Who knows what he might do, if he gets out. I'm counting on ya. We must protect Lore."

Monk turns his attention to the glutinous mixture.

Borj finds the shut-off valve for the water. When he returns, the mixture is a solid cylinder. There is no escape for Disposal-Man.

"What happens next?" asks Monk.

"I'll call the city. They can figure out what to do with him. We've done our part. We stopped him."

By two in the morning, The Flour Mill is surrounded by city officials, police, paramedics and firemen. The harlequin light from the first-responder vehicles dances across the ground. Floodlights, arranged by firemen, bathe the silo in light. Workers have attached a cable from a gargantuan, heavy-lift crane to the block of papier-mâché. The crane engine roars and the cable strains, hoisting the monstrous mass from the silo.

"We did a good job," pronounces Borj. He swings a hardened papier-mâché arm over Monk's shoulder.

Carefully, the crane operator lowers the block onto a flatbed truck where workers secure the monolith.

With lights flashing, a convoy of vehicles head to The Millhouse.

"Time for us to go," says Monk. "They could have at least offered a ride."

"I asked. They said they couldn't. Insurance doesn't cover transporting civilians. We're on our own."

Finally, a tow truck leaves, pulling the tractor and wagon.

"Tractor's dead," Monk observes.

"No buses this time of night," adds Borj. "You up for a walk?"

"Looks like it," answers Monk. "I'm not cut out for this superhero stuff. There must be a better way. What about you?"

"On days like this, I love what I do."

Borj and Monk make the long walk back into the city center where they part company.

Borj picks up an early edition of the Lickspittle.

Worn-out, Borj reaches his apartment where cuts himself out of his costume. With a little work, he can salvage his boots. His cape will need a new 'B'. The old one was lost when Disposal-Man tore the cape. The rest of his costume is ruined. Fortunately, he has spare costume parts.

Borj showers and climbs into his pajamas.

He reads the lead article on the front-page of the newspaper: Chaos in Middleman. The article heavily criticizes Borj and his unknown assistant. Their reckless behavior has left a trail of property damage throughout the suburb, endangered the lives of countless Loreans, and left taxpayers on the hook for the costs associated with the disposal of Disposal-Man. Borj throws the newspaper into a corner of the room.

He writes in his journal about the day's experiences.

Turning on the radio, he drifts off to sleep while listening to *Sweet Dreams (Are Made of This)*.

Meanwhile, the crane operator, police and prison officials unload the papier-mâché plug into The Millhouse prison facility.

Isn't It Obvious?

Three years after Disposal-Man's capture, a motor scooter navigates through the streets of Lore. Borj's mode of transport is an amalgam of rusting components that he has cobbled together into the semblance of a scooter. The frame he found in a curbside junk pile in the once-prosperous suburb of Middleman.

Block after city block lies empty. The paper and plastic jetsam of Lore tumbles through the deserted streets, finding temporary homes pressed against chain-link fencing and boarded-up buildings. Most Loreans have gone to the coalfields of New Grubbeemitts in Pawsoff. Much of the city's infrastructure has failed. The transit system, including the subway, stopped running a year ago. Disposal-Man remains incarcerated in The Millhouse, trapped in his papier-mâché prison.

The Lickspittle Free Press doggedly continues to publish despite an almost nonexistent readership. The owners of the newspaper had the foresight decades ago to negotiate a contract with The Millhouse to print and distribute the paper. At the time, Loreans expressed concern about prisoners roaming city streets delivering the newspaper to newsstands. The owners of the Lickspittle convinced the citizens that the day-parole program was a positive way to re-integrate inmates into open society. Now, bundles of newspapers pile up at deserted newsstands.

Only a few hundred Loreans inhabit the inner city. Reliable numbers are hard to ascertain. Those who remain have barricaded themselves in their apartments. Emerging only when dwindling supplies dictate, they scurry about in the shadows, scrounging for ever scarcer commodities (primarily food and water) to sustain their meager existence. They, like Borj, are unwilling to abandon the city. Most of them seem harmless.

In the dusk of twilight, Borj halts his scooter beside the corroding remains of a car. This stop is one of many he has made today in his hunt for gasoline. If unsuccessful this time, he will need to wait until tomorrow before he can resume his search.

Hunkering down beside the fill pipe, he inserts a hose and manages to coax a trickle of the precious liquid into a scrounged gas can. Relieved, he hopes there's enough to keep his scooter going for a few days, if he rations carefully. He watches the thin stream intently and ignores the creeping darkness.

"You're the scooter guy, aren't ya?" asks a man, stepping out from behind the car.

Borj snaps a quick look over his shoulder at the tall lanky stranger. He gets a sinking feeling in the pit of his stomach. A pump-action shotgun rests on the man's hip. The handle of a nine-millimeter pistol protrudes from a shoulder holster. Nearly all remaining Loreans have armed themselves. Borj and a few others are exceptions. Why had the man approached? You had to size up people fast in this stark environment. He hopes the man is only looking for some company, or wanting to trade information: an old currency. It must have taken guts for him to approach. Borj focuses his attention on siphoning gas.

"Most of us call ya Scooter." The man is a little jumpy. He scans the nearby, abandoned vehicles that might offer cover to a would-be assailant. "Not much gas left these days. You're lucky to find any. Might be stale though," he conjectures.

"Yeah," Borj casually replies, suppressing his fear. Events could quickly spiral out of control were he to send the wrong signal. "Ya look familiar. What's your name?" Borj inquires, deciding to take a chance. Loreans who have turned survivalist like their anonymity and are, by nature, distrustful.

"Healer. They call me Healer. This used to be a good neighborhood," he adds. "I grew up here." He looks carefully about, appraising the seemingly uninhabited street.

"Healer, that's an interesting name. Where did ya get it?" Borj wants to keep the conversation going. Sometimes putting a human face to things helps dispel tension. He prefers talking to ease a situation. "You a doctor?"

"I was a paramedic before this." He waves his shotgun at the looming dark, as though trying to ward it off. The streetlights have not worked for many months. "A first responder when people needed help," he proudly adds. At no time does he look at the vulnerable Borj.

Borj wonders if Healer is nervous about what might happen in the darkness—there are rumors—or maybe Healer is trying to look out for a neighbor. Or possibly he's thinking about what he plans to do once it's dark.

"Ya almost finished?" He sounds impatient. "You're compromised here. Ya make an easy target. Ya should at least arm yourself."

"Almost done." Borj doesn't want to get drawn into a debate about firearms. In Borj's mind, guns make the mix more volatile, not less so. He wishes the gas would flow faster.

"Why haven't ya left like the others?" Healer asks.

These loners don't like to share scarce resources, and leaving the city would mean one less competitor for diminishing supplies. Does Healer want Borj to leave Lore, or does he want to understand why Borj stays on, like himself? Maybe Healer is looking for common ground with someone who has decided to remain. Maybe he wants to know how committed Borj is. Perhaps he's sizing up Borj as a potential ally. Borj doesn't know which angle Healer is working. Maybe Healer wants the gas and is willing to do whatever it takes to get it.

"Don't know," answers Borj. "Maybe the same reason you stay," Borj offers. "Why are ya here?" he queries, hoping to elicit an insight into his own reluctance to leave.

"What?" Healer is bewildered by Borj's question. "Isn't it obvious?" Healer replies. "Are ya done?" he asks, looking at the gas can.

"Almost."

"There are rumors of a gang roaming this area," Healer cautions. "They drive around in old cars, black ones. If they catch ya siphoning gas, they're not going to like it. This is their turf. I hear the gang is led by an old guy driving a two-door coupe. According to the rumors, his name is Jobber. Don't trust him. They say he's harmless, but people disappear after he shows up. At least that's what I hear. I haven't seen him. My cousin met a guy once who knew a woman, who dated a guy a couple of times, who was supposed to be one of Jobber's gang. I think his name was Slash. If ya see him, be careful."

"Thanks." answers Borj, troubled by the tenuous six-degrees of separation. Did Jobber and his sidekick, Slash, really exist, or were they a Lorean myth; folk devils? Borj couldn't remember reading anything in the Lickspittle Free Press. However, you couldn't trust the paper at the best of times. Although, you would expect that, if there was a smidgen of truth to the rumor, the Lickspittle would have sucked it up and slapped it on the front page in at least some mangled form of the truth: Missing Loreans Abducted by Head Hunters!

"I haven't seen them. I'll keep a lookout," replies Borj, trying to be cooperative. A dismissive response would be the wrong tack, a lack of respect. And sometimes the truth is more bizarre than fiction.

"I thought maybe ya might have seen these guys. Ya have wheels, a scooter. At least I think it's a scooter," observes Healer, appraising Borj's mode of transportation.

"Ya cover more territory. Ya likely see more than I do. It pays to stay in touch."

"If I see anything, I'll let ya know." Borj is uncertain how he might contact Healer should the need arise.

The gas slows to an intermittent drip.

"If you're running low on supplies, let me know," Borj volunteers, while concentrating on getting every drop. "Maybe I can find what you're looking for. Do you need anything in the way of supplies?"

There is no response.

"There, that should do it," adds Borj to fill the silence. He pulls the hose from the fill pipe, stands up and turns around, looking for an answer.

Healer has disappeared.

Borj never saw or heard from him again. There was an unconfirmed report that Healer was ambushed by the Jobber guy. Borj couldn't verify the story in those garbled times.

As he had done prior to his encounter with Healer, Borj continues to ask himself why he stays. A satisfactory answer eludes him, fostered by a sense that there is something not done that... That what? His thought trails off, unable to comprehend what it is that is playing out and tenaciously refuses to let go.

Who Knew?

A couple of months after the encounter with Healer, Borj's scooter navigates a deserted avenue. The wind rattles and rolls an empty beer can down the sidewalk. The Millhouse Brewing Company has relocated to Pawsoff, and rebranded itself as the Grubbeemitts Brewing Company.

'T-ting t-ting t-ting…' cheerfully hails the aluminum vessel at Borj's passing scooter.

'Rrrrrip, rrrrrip, rrrrrrrrrip,' confidently counters the scooter. Steering through a jumble of abandoned vehicles, it speeds away, leaving the container to continue alone on its journey.

'Flap, flap,' waves Borj's cape. Unable to afford a new cape, he wears the same one worn the day he faced Disposal-Man.

Following the daily routine, the scooter pulls up next to the curb in front of the building that still houses the National Protection Agency (NPA). Borj cuts the engine, dismounts, and jerks the scooter onto its stand. He removes his orange, half helmet, and riding goggles and hangs them on a handle bar.

He pushes through a building door. The booth previously occupied by Cornelius is empty. He vanished without a trace a short while after the capture of Disposal-Man. Borj unlocks the agency door. The agency dismissed the security guards a year ago. They were no longer needed.

He jams his time card into the punch clock and puts it in the 'In' rack. His is the only card in the rack and will remain so.

Borj walks into the agency waiting room. A phone remains on the floor where Lydia's desk used to be. Lydia left of her own accord and was not replaced. The agency reassigned Clay to the downtown headquarters. His dedication to NPA goals, hard work and expertise with charts and graphs had finally paid off. Clay was ecstatic about the promotion. Later, due to lack of business, the agency downsized and reorganized, leaving Clay to seek employment elsewhere. Stapes and P-Cut went missing two years ago. They gave no notice. Their whereabouts are unknown.

Borj picks up the phone and listens for a dial tone.

'Nnnnnnnn,' replies the phone as if to say, 'Yep I'm still here. What can I do for you?'

Satisfied, Borj hangs up. Shortly after Clay's departure, an NPA employee phoned the office. The voice sounded familiar. The caller informed Borj that he was to answer the phone, if it rang. NPA would contact him, if it had an assignment for him. Although he had not heard from the agency since, the company continued to pay his meager salary.

Borj studies the SV write-ups on the walls. Most of the villains have disappeared, except for a few minor evil doers (for instance, Bubble-Gum-Guy). Criminals, such as Hyperbole-Man and Enabler-Man, who relied on their ability to influence the people of Lore to achieve their ends, fell on hard times, the result of the shrinking population. Eventually, most SVs relocated to cities that offered more lucrative opportunities. They continue to play the same old games for their own diabolical ends: world domination, or vengeance for some real or imagined slight.

'Chirp, chirp,' sings the ever-optimistic phone, startling Borj. He picks up the receiver.

"Hello, NPA."

"Hi. The Lickspittle Free Press is offering free home delivery. Are ya interested?"

"No thanks," Borj answers. "This line must be kept open. Please don't call this number again."

'Nnnnnn,' responds the phone.

The hour hand on the office clock scrapes onward. Tired of studying fact sheets for SVs that no longer pose a threat, Borj plays solitaire to pass the time. Lunch time comes and goes. The afternoon drags by.

'Chirp, chirp,' warbles the phone, waking the dozing Borj. He picks up the phone.

"Hello," he answers groggily.

"Hey, kid. How's it going? Ya weren't sleeping on the job were ya?"

"No, no."

"Never mind. I got a job for ya. I need ya to step outside."

"Yeah, sure," Borj answers. "Who is this?"

"It's me. I said I'd call if I had anything. Well I got a proposition for ya. Step outside and I'll tell ya about it."

"Isn't this kind of cloak and dagger? Why not come inside?"

"Meet me outside."

'Nnnnnn,' says the phone.

Surmising that he is about to be downsized, Borj takes one last look at the office before leaving.

He waits by the curb. The street is empty. There is no sign of anyone.

Must be a prank call, he concludes after about fifteen minutes.

He is about to step back into the building when a black car the size of a rhino charges around a corner, swerves toward the curb and bulldozes his scooter into scrap metal. Unscathed, the vehicle veers to the middle of the road and slowly rumbles by Borj. The windows are tinted, making it impossible to see inside the car. The vehicle rolls to a stop a half-dozen car lengths up the street, where it continues to idle. No one gets out. Borj coolly watches to see what will happen next. Several equally hulking cars roll up behind the first vehicle and stop. The muffled sound of music emanates from the coupe in the middle. The lead driver cuts the engine and two men dressed as convicts get out.

Well, who knew? ponders the astonished Borj.

And What I Will Is Fate

Stapes and P-Cut reconnoiter the area. P-Cut signals the all-clear. The drivers in the remaining vehicles cut their engines. Heavily armed men exit the cars flanking the coupe. Stapes approaches the car. He raps on the tinted window of the driver's door. The door springs open. Music explodes from the vehicle. The Rolling Stones are singing about someone not getting any satisfaction. The driver launches into a fiery one-sided argument that Borj can't hear over the music. His view of the occupant is blocked.

What next? Can it get any better? Borj wonders.

The driver launches himself out of the vehicle. It's Cornelius. He's wearing a black watch cap, t-shirt and pants and his signature running shoes. On his t-shirt is the message 'And what I will is fate.' He tosses a stone-faced nod of recognition at Borj, who reciprocates with a smile.

Unbelievable, I guess it can get better, Borj decides.

Several men haul mats from the trunk of a car and lay them flat on the road. Cornelius oversees their efforts, barking orders until he's satisfied with the arrangement.

Concentrating, Cornelius signals with a nod. Immediately, The Rolling Stones stop. There's a pause while he limbers up with an impromptu moonwalk. He stops. Now deep in concentration, he signals his readiness with the nod of his head. A new song, *I Will Not Serve*, explodes from the car speakers. He leaps into a series of break-dance moves in time with the detonation of the heart-stopping music that shakes his car. He starts with a 'Microburst' that he extends into a 'Dead-Man Bounce', followed by a 'Train Wreck', 'Coffee Grinder', and more. Finally, he spins to a stop, lying prone on the mats. On cue, the music stops. Stapes gives him a hand up. P-Cut congratulates him on his performance and offers him a cigarillo, which he accepts. Stapes provides a light. Smiling, Cornelius walks over to Borj.

"Ya like that last move, kid? I call it the 'No-name Ambush'. I added it special for ya. Been working on it for a month. That's my signature move."

"That's pretty good for an old guy," Borj observes. "Who taught ya that one?"

Cornelius glares. "What do ya mean taught? Who do ya think created it?"

He surveys the remains of the wrecked scooter. "That your bike? What happened to it? Never mind. It doesn't matter. Ya don't need it. Ya can ride with me."

"What brings ya here?"

"I got an assignment for ya. Ya interested? Course ya are."

"Why were ya in the booth handing out ID badges?"

"I like to go undercover to see how things are going. Stands to reason, doesn't it? Have to keep an eye on my investment. It's just common sense."

"You're the agency?"

"Yep, always have been and a lot more too, a hobby of mine. Ya going to stand here and gab all day? I got things to do. Time is money. Let's go. We can talk on the way."

"I better lock up the agency first," Borj responds. He is hesitant to get in the coupe.

"Forget it. Get in," orders Cornelius, disappearing into the car.

Borj wavers for a moment before getting in on the passenger side.

'Thud,' says the car door, closing beside him.

Borj searches for a seat belt.

Cornelius starts the engine and cranks up the music. A singer wails about insurrection and the loneliness of prison.

Cornelius puts the car in gear. He lays on the horn to get the others moving.

"What are ya looking for? Never mind a frigging seat belt. Ya won't find one. They're an infringement on my freedom."

He punches the horn again. "Come on, let's go!" he bellows at the windshield. He steps on the gas. The coupe snarls and leaps forward in tandem with the other cars. Bending to his will, the vehicle flies through the narrow streets.

"Where are we headed?" Borj yells over the music.

"Downtown. Where else would we be going?" Cornelius guns the engine, swings wide, jumps the curb and turns down a side street. The car yelps in protest.

"Why me?" Borj asks, hanging on tight.

"Why not you? You're no different than anyone else. I'm giving ya a ride is all. It doesn't mean anything. Don't let it go to your head."

"What about Stapes and P-Cut?"

"Who? Never heard of them. Holy hell, what kind of name is P-Cut anyway? Sounds like somebody pissed himself and ripped off a fart. And the other guy, what's his name?"

"Stapes," yells Borj.

"Sounds like some half-assed, office boy," hollers Cornelius, the veins in his neck standing out. The truth is it's totally the wrong image, if ya want to do merc work for me. Makes me look bad, no style. Style is everything ya know. If ya roll with me, ya better look the part."

"They're the two guys in the lead vehicle."

"Oh, those idiots! Why didn't ya say so? They wanted work, so I gave them jobs and new names too. Let me think. What did I call them? Oh yeah, Slash and Razor. Hang on." Cornelius warns, as he sends the car careening around another corner. The centripetal force pushes Borj hard against the door. "Come on, faster!" he yells at the windshield. "Did ya notice the prisoner uniforms I make them wear? I developed them up at The Millhouse. And no, I didn't do time in The Millhouse, if that's what you're thinking. I'm an entrepreneur in case ya hadn't noticed."

"Which did ya develop at The Millhouse, Slash and Razor or the uniforms?"

"What? Pay attention! The uniforms of course."

"Kind of ironic, isn't it?" hollers Borj.

"Ironic?"

"Well, they're supposed to be free men, Slash and Razor.

"Yeah, so?

"Ya dress them like convicts."

"I don't get it. Never mind. Focus. I have a whole line of prisoner attire. That's what's important. Branded the lot with the Millhouse logo. Did ya notice?"

"Ya mean the eagle on top of the 'ME' letters? What's that thing in its talons?"

"For your information, it's not an eagle. It's a falcon that's nailed a crow. The branding adds value, style. Most buy the stuff just for the logo. Gives them a sense of status. Makes them feel like they belong to something big. The line generates lots of revenue. I used to make it in The Millhouse till I found cheaper offshore labor."

The coupe slams around another corner.

"Slow down! Riding with you is like riding in the ass end of a cement mixer. Ya got a death wish?"

"Relax. You're in good hands. I won't steer ya wrong. Get it, steer ya wrong?"

"What's merc work?"

"Yeah, ya know, merc work. Holy hell! Where ya been? They're mercenaries. They work for me under contract. They're responsible for their own benefits, cuts down on paperwork."

Cornelius steps hard on the gas. The car races down a main street. He ignores the few traffic lights that are working, blowing through red light after red light. Borj braces himself with his back jammed against the seat and his feet hard against the floorboard.

"Loosen up. I've made this run lots of times without a scratch." The speed demon smiles at Borj in a gesture of reassurance.

Borj gasps in crazy-eyed terror. He jams his feet harder into the floorboard, looking for a nonexistent brake pedal.

The vehicle leaps onto the sidewalk and slams into a derelict newsstand that explodes into a hundred pieces. The hulking vehicle flies on, taking out everything in its path. Cornelius wrestles the beast back onto the road.

"See, not a scratch. This monster is built like a tank," he proudly announces.

"Which one is Slash and which one Razor?" Borj persists, returning to his earlier question. He fights the urge to leap out of the car.

"Holy hell, what do I look like, a frigging encyclopedia? I don't know and I don't care. They both answer when I call. It doesn't matter which name I use. And I don't give a damn anyway. When I tell them to come, they come. They run errands for me. Ya know. Run and get a copy of the Lickspittle. Ya read the Lickspittle? I own it. Own most of this city. Course it's dying now. That's okay. I got other plans: moving the whole operation to Pawsoff."

"Are you the guy that God supposedly raptured a few years ago?"

"Raptured my ass! That's the last thing that's going to happen to me! Where did ya get that shit anyway, the Lickspittle? I had to admire the Editor for that one. What balls! He showed initiative and that's a rare quality in my minions. He thought it up all by himself and did it. I like that. Promoted him for printing that lie. Damn good one too. Gave away lots of papers that day. Boosted advertising for months. Now he's responsible for my entire newspaper chain. I'm a conglomerate ya know. I'm into everything.

Ya name it, I own it and that includes The Millhouse. I'm ME."

Borj looks out the window. The car rockets by The Millhouse. "Ya own it?"

"What did I just say? Of course I do! Have for a long time, forever almost. I have a contract with the government. They send me the scum of the earth and I lock them up. It's a good system: efficient. Ya know what a millhouse is?"

"Place where ya grind wheat into flour, isn't it?"

"Yeah that's right. Lots of things get ground up. That's enough chitchat. Quiet now. I'm concentrating on my driving."

A few minutes later, the cars pull up in front of the Millhouse Plaza with its dozen or so skyscrapers. The plaza is deserted. Cornelius hits the brakes. The vehicle comes to a screaming stop, throwing Borj forward. With a reflexive jerk of his arm, his hand slams into the dashboard. Piston-like, his arm decelerates his forward momentum, avoiding an unwelcome tête-à-tête. His lead-foot chauffeur is oblivious to the near encounter. Cornelius shuts off the music.

"We're here," he states, hopping out of the car without further explanation. "What are ya waiting for?" he demands, peering back into the vehicle. "Get up off your ass. Bail out, thirty-thousand feet," he commands, as if talking to a paratrooper. He bangs shut his door.

Borj scrambles out of the coupe. He falls in line a pace behind Cornelius, who does a quick march with his dozen or so subordinates trailing in lockstep.

"Your posse always this big?"

"There's strength in numbers. I've made a few enemies along the way. It's only natural. Enemies I mean."

"Where are we going?"

"You'll see."

"Ya move fast," observes Borj, trying to keep up with his speedy host, who seems to have reached terminal velocity.

78

Intent on his purpose, Cornelius ignores Borj.

Slash and Razor race ahead. Holding open the doors to the main building, they wait as their leader and his followers rumble by.

"They're with me," snarls Cornelius without further explanation as he strides by a security guard.

The guard responds with a nervous nod. He presses a button on his desk. Security doors fly open. The phalanx of bodies slides through and heads to a bank of elevators.

What Else Is There?

"Get in," Cornelius orders, stepping into an elevator. "The rest of ya wait here. We got business to discuss. I'll be back."

Borj steps in. With the hum of hidden machinery, the doors close behind him. The elevator begins its ascent. Somewhere in the walls, someone is singing about battles lost and won.

"What do ya think?" Cornelius gestures at the walls. "Ya like it?"

"Roomy. Not much of a view though. How long have you and your gang been running Lore? It's seen better days."

"Gang! There's no gang. I'm a legitimate corporation. Use your head! Who do ya think built this place?" he sputters, launching a volley of spittle at Borj. "Who do ya think keeps it going? And not only Lore! There's a lot more. Think outside the box, will ya? I'm amazed that ya can't see the truth and appreciate what I've done. Ya don't get it!" He wipes his mouth with a wadded-up rag and angrily stuffs it back into his pants pocket.

"I didn't mean a criminal gang. I meant a gang of workers, subordinates."

"Ya read much?" Cornelius asks. "Ya should read. It's good for ya, culture and all that shit. How else ya going to get culture? Lifts the spirit, makes ya feel good about who ya are. Ya ever read *Paradise Lost*?"

Borj shakes his head no, unsure where this conversation is going.

"Not a bad poem. Written by a guy named Milton. Not like the stuff ya read today, cheap tabloids and stuff ya watch on TV. Milton's poem has a richness to it, texture, especially the first couple of chapters. Ya know what I'm saying? He's got lots to say even if he doesn't always get it right. Worse than the Lickspittle in some places," he says, scowling. "Stuff nowadays never looks below the surface, at least not most of it. Oh, there are a few writers that look, though not many. Anyway, ya should try *Paradise Lost*. Ya got a lot in common with the hero of the story."

"How so?"

"Both of ya have fallen on hard times through no fault of your own. Remember, never underestimate your enemy. That's a lesson I learned the hard way. I've been paying for it ever since."

"What enemy?"

A new song, *John the Revelator*, drifts from an overhead speaker mounted in the wall.

"Holy shit! That's disgusting. This isn't the gospel hour. Who put on that crap? Good help is hard to find."

Cornelius reaches into his pocket and pulls out a slim, gold-plated device.

"See this? I call it my zapper. Works like a TV remote control. It's real handy. Great for changing channels on electronic stuff. Works on other stuff too. Maybe I'll show ya later. Watch this." He aims the device at the speaker. "And zap," he adds for dramatic effect, pressing a button.

The singer persists, undaunted by the attempt to silence him.

"Well, ya son of a…" He shoves the zapper back into his pocket. "Give me a boost," Cornelius demands, lifting a foot so Borj can push him up.

Borj stares in disbelief.

"Come on! What are ya waiting for? Give me a boost up or get down on all fours. I don't care which. When I tell ya to do something, ya do it. Now move! Get with the program."

Against his better judgment, Borj pushes him up.

"That's better. Next time, move faster."

With the side of his face mashed against Cornelius' rear end, Borj can't see what's happening. He can hear pounding on the speaker. The singer continues.

"Bugger!" growls Cornelius. He rips the speaker out of the wall with his bare hands and drops it. It dangles from a couple of wires. "Quiet!" he barks."

The singer croons on about John the Revelator.

"Well, ya piece a…" Preempting the singer, he rips the speaker free of its wires and throws it to the floor. The speaker is silent. "That's better. Never liked that song. Let me down. What are ya waiting for? Get your ass in gear!" he orders.

Borj lowers him to the floor.

"It's okay. I own the building," Cornelius explains to set Borj's mind at rest about the damage. "Sorry about that. The music I mean. It won't happen again."

The elevator stops and the doors slide open.

"Follow me," orders Borj's tour guide, motioning with his hand, "this way. You're going to like this." He forces a welcoming smile and steps onto a landing, followed by Borj.

The elevator shuts its doors and descends.

"Look, we're here." Cornelius beams, holding open the door to the rooftop. "Come on! I haven't got all day! What do I look like, a doorman? Move it!" He motions with his free hand. A sudden gust of wind grabs the door. He resists.

"For someone as ancient as you, you're incredibly strong," responds Borj, stepping onto the roof.

"Yeah yeah, stand clear," warns Cornelius, releasing the door.

Borj leaps forward to avoid being hit.

'BANG!' barks the door, slamming shut.

"I only got twenty minutes for this, so pay attention."

"We're not locked out, are we?"

"There's nothing to worry about. I can leave any time."

"What are we doing here?"

"Come on," hollers Cornelius over the buffeting wind that seems intent on snatching away his words.

Leaning against the force of the wind, the old man walks to the railing that wraps around the perimeter of the roof. His forward progress is jerky, owing to the variable wind gusts. Reaching the railing, he grasps it with both hands. Beyond, the building drops straight down ninety stories.

"Don't ya love it? I like to… What are ya doing back there?" he yells in disbelief. Borj hasn't joined him. "Ya can't see nothing back there. Get over here!" He swats impatiently at the air, motioning Borj to join him. Cornelius begins to wonder if Borj is a little dull witted. "Jeeze, the things I put up with! What are ya afraid of?"

Reluctantly, Borj joins him. He peers down at the ground below.

"See, it's safe," says Cornelius, giving the railing a good shake to demonstrate its reliability.

"I wouldn't do that, if I were you."

"Ya got nothing to worry about." He looks up at Borj through his thick round glasses. "I like ya, kid. Can ya work with me?"

"Sure, what are we doing here?"

"This," states Cornelius, looking at the scene below. Beneath them are greasy-gray rooftops; modern skyscrapers with bile-green, glass windows; and scrimshawed streets extending in all directions. "See that canal over there?" he notes as a special point of interest. "I built that," he adds with pride.

Borj peers at the remains of what was once a river. It's squeezed into a canal lined on both sides by enormous buildings. He loses sight of the waterway. When next glimpsed at the city's edge, the sluggish water has shed its cement liner in favor of tree-lined banks.

Below him, Borj spots a helicopter, thrashing its way above the rooftops. It's following the main traffic artery leading into the city's core. The helicopter's windshield reminds him of the compound eyes of a dragonfly. A red, running light winks knowingly.

'Thud, thud, thud,' faintly call the rotor blades of the resolute helicopter.

"What's it doing here?" asks Borj, pointing toward the helicopter. A gust of wind roars across the rooftop, snatching away his question. He tightens his grip on the rail.

Relaxed, Cornelius leans against the rail. Lost in wonder, he stares at the once-thriving and now almost empty metropolis, a small corner of his ME empire. "I love coming up here. Inspiring, isn't it? I enjoy looking at what I've created with these two hands." He reaches out momentarily, as though trying to scoop up the world with his calloused hands, the kind you might expect of someone who has spent many lives doing manual labor.

Where did he get those hands? Borj speculates. *There isn't much need for manual labor in Lore, except in The Millhouse and even there not so much.*

Borj glances up and down at Cornelius, who is unaware of Borj's examination. His body is lean and rock hard. His blanched skin looks like an old business suit that's been blowing around in a desert for countless millennia.

Who are ya old man? Borj wonders. *What hell-hole did ya come from?*

Marveling at the view, Cornelius smiles, takes a deep breath, pauses, and then slowly exhales. "Renews my sense of purpose, my destiny. Yeah, that's it, destiny. Ya know what I mean? Reminds me why I'm here. Did ya ever get that feeling, that wondering why you're here? And ya know the answer, don't ya? The reality is ya know for a certainty, deep in your bones. It's a wonderful feeling knowing. Isn't it? Ya know why you're here, right?" he asks, looking with hard searching eyes at Borj.

"Ya mean here now? This isn't some sort of hearts-and-minds speech, is it?" Borj asks suspiciously.

"Hearts and minds! Are ya shitting me? I won that war long ago. That's pathetic. Maybe I've misjudged ya. Ya know your fate is already sealed, right? Ya made a choice. Ya have to live with it. The reality is there's no redemption! Makes for a good story though," he adds, "the idea ya can trade in all this for a better life. Well, ya got your religion anyway. I like to think of it as a faint-hope clause. Religion, I mean. Keeps ya trying, well sort of. For most, it's a half-assed try. Why would ya want to give up all this? What's the alternative? Ya may as well see what ya can make of yourself because that's all there is, nothing more, only the here and now. Enjoy what ya can while ya can. You're a long-time dead."

"Then why are we here?" asks Borj, trying to extract meaning from the grist ground by his would-be mentor.

"I'm beginning to think maybe I made a mistake bringing ya here," says Cornelius, looking with skepticism at Borj. "Why it's the economy. What else is there? It's a beautiful piece of machinery, a well-oiled machine. It's all right here in front of your face." He spreads his arms, gesturing at the city below. "Slickest shit ever invented, all in the interest of..." He lets the sentence trail off, having caught himself on the verge of saying too much. "It's a very practical way for distributing wealth, giving everyone their due. It's all so wonderfully indifferent. Of course, ya have to earn your piece of the pie and there's never enough. 'Blessed are they that hunger and thirst' for they shall be satisfied. There's motivation for ya. I wish I'd thought up that line. I love it. Ya follow me?" Cornelius looks at Borj's eyes. He places a fatherly hand on Borj's shoulder.

Borj resists the urge to flinch. His cape tugs in the wind.

"Are ya sure about that hunger and thirst? It doesn't sound right to me the way ya say it."

"I'm sure. Trust me. I know."

"Sounds like it's missing something."

"Nope it's all there. Anyway, down to business." Cornelius looks at his watch. "We haven't got much time left. What are ya looking for out of life: money, women, fame? What is it ya want?"

"Are ya expecting someone?"

"Never mind that. I'm here to help ya. In case ya hadn't noticed, Lore is dead. It's time for ya to move on. Why don't ya come and work for me? I don't mean NPA. I'm closing down the agency effective immediately."

"Does that mean I'm fired?"

"Nope, it's only a permanent layoff. Don't take it personally. It's just business. And besides, I'm always looking for people that are creative, people like you. I like the way ya got rid of thingamajig-man."

"Ya mean Disposal-Man?"

"Whatever. Ya showed imagination and guts too. I can use someone like you. I'm opening a new company in Pawsoff to protect the people from the super villains that have started sniffing around. I'm looking for someone to help run the new agency. Be my boots on the ground ya might say, the second assault wave hitting the beach. I sent the first wave centuries ago. They were mostly intel: intelligence gatherers. They've been sending back reports ever since. Ya wouldn't start at the top. Still, with your experience, ya could work your way up damn fast. No more fighting in the trenches. I could start ya in a branch office as a manager. Do graphs and charts, report to head office, shit like that. Ya could sit in your office and send others out to do the grunt work. Naturally ya would get more money each time ya climb a link in the food chain. ME can be very generous, if ya got the right stuff. Stands to reason, doesn't it? The higher ya go, the more responsibility ya have and the more money ya get. It's common sense. I'm offering ya a plum job. There are lots of other people, like Slash and Razor, that would jump at the chance. Problem is, they don't have the right stuff."

"They're a little rough around the edges. They could learn. They need a little prodding in the right direction, like the rest of us."

"See, now you're thinking like a manager, assessing the abilities of your assets. Ya would need to be a little hard-assed at times. Ya can learn that. Then all ya need is a little faith in me. I'm doing this for your own good and the good of others too. Ya want to hire Slash and Razor? Sure, go ahead. It's up to you. You're running the office. If ya turn a profit, things are good. I mean, it's only fair that I get a decent return on my investment. Ya get a base salary and the rest would be a bonus based on performance, an incentives program. Don't worry about that for now. We can work out the details later. What do ya think?"

"It's a long way…"

"Yeah yeah, I know. It's a long way from family and friends," interrupts Cornelius. "Look, Pawsoff is kind of a wild west, a lawless place. They're a lot of bad people there. The fact of the matter is, ya can't trust anyone. Ya wouldn't want to take family with ya, at least not right away. Ya got a kid sister right, Joki? Maybe in a few years she can join ya after things settle in, if you're still thinking that's what ya want. And ya won't have time for relatives anyway. Sure as shit, it'll take all your time and energy getting the office up and running. So, do ya trust that I'm doing the right thing for ya? I'm trying to help ya because I like ya. Ya got potential. I'm only trying to help ya realize it, give ya a little guidance. Know what I mean?"

A gust of wind pulls urgently at Borj's cape.

"Course ya would be required to follow corporate policy. Hell, ya can even write the policy for all I care."

"Policy isn't my strong suit," answers Borj, bewildered by the course of the conversation. "I hadn't thought about…"

"Ah, I'm only shitting ya," Cornelius interjects. "Maybe ya would have some influence on policy making. Let's see how it goes first. Ya interested? An opening like this doesn't hammer on your door every day. It's like winning the lottery."

Cornelius wets a finger and holds it up. The wind has momentarily subsided.

"Ya think about it for a minute while I take a piss." He unzips his fly. "I'm watering the economy," he observes while peeing over the edge of the precipice. "I'm giving ya a practical demonstration. Pay attention. I'm making things grow." He hums a popular tune, *Got the World by the Balls*. He chuckles, setting off one of his red-in-the-face coughing fits, like there's a clod of dirt stuck in his throat. He fights to maintain control. "See." he says, having recovered. "This is how it's done."

A sudden blast of wind sweeps up the side of the building.

"Ah, holy shit!" says Cornelius with a look of revulsion. The front of his pants and shirt are wet. "Son of a…" He zips up. "Damn!"

Borj stifles a laugh.

"What are ya laughing at?"

"Give it a minute. It'll dry," says Borj, trying to hide a smile, and feeling that for the first time he has made a useful contribution to the conversation.

"What's your answer, kid? Are ya with me? What's it going to be?" he demands, brushing his shirt and pants with brusque strokes.

"I don't think that's the right…"

"You're like the rest of them, aren't ya?" shouts Cornelius, abandoning his brushing. "Ya think there's more. Makes ya weak," he accuses. "Your weakness is my strength. There isn't more. This is all there is. Ya want people to be decent, trustworthy and caring," he appends with a sneer. Impulsively, he jams a hand into a pants pocket and pulls out his remote control. He flips it from hand to hand, making it spin in the air. "Ya want them to carry themselves with dignity and that won't happen. Ya want them to be…"

His lecture is cut short by the roar of a helicopter, rising alongside the building. The machine clears the roofline. A brutal whirlwind hurls loose rooftop gravel at Borj and Cornelius, who ignores the abrasive blast, intent on what is about to transpire. The copter continues its ascent, moving into position above them.

Shielding his face from the rasping stones, Borj looks up to see what is happening.

"Your ride is here," Cornelius bellows to be heard above the chop of the blades. "I was going to send ya to Pawsoff. Now I don't think so."

"What?" yells Borj. "What's going on? I can't hear ya."

"Ever been to sea?" Cornelius presses a couple of buttons on his zapper. "Time ya had a change of scenery." He aims the device at Borj and presses a button.

Borj slumps to the roof. The winch operator in the copter lowers a harness. Slipping the harness over the unconscious Borj, Cornelius pulls it tight, steps away, and gives a thumbs-up. The operator hoists Borj into the machine. It hovers momentarily, turns and flies off, becoming a distant dot and finally disappearing.

"That should hold him," mutters Cornelius. He steps back into the building, satisfied with a good day's work.

'BANG!' The door slams behind him.

The Dancing Walrus

Tom Booker, a reporter for the Lickspittle Free Press, stands beside a sculpture known to the residents of The Millhouse as The Dancing Walrus. The statue in all its glory is the transformed block of papier-mâché in which Disposal-Man remains a prisoner. Everything about the Walrus is in motion. Carefully balanced on a hind flipper, formed from the pallets that Borj stapled to Disposal-Man's boots, the Walrus looks amazingly agile and free, oblivious to its bulk and surroundings. Even the flipper looks ready to take flight. The Walrus appears to be in another realm.

A Millhouse prison guard, Barr, stands close by Tom in the common area used by the inmates. Barr is a "newbie" in the detention system, having joined the staff when his job at NPA was declared redundant. Most of the guards have worked in The Millhouse for twenty or more years. Barr, in contrast, has served only a year and, more importantly, was hired without the proper family background. There is an understanding that a candidate for the job requires a family connection to someone (for example, a father or aunt) who holds one of the coveted positions in the prison. Hiring an applicant with a familial tie gives the newbie a better understanding of the organization, how it functions and how to carry oneself within the prison structure during the normal course of one's time in the facility. Beginning in earliest childhood, there are rules and lessons that are intentionally and accidentally (mostly accidentally) inculcated to children by their parents, or close relatives. For example, the tried and true 'trust only family members' translates in the penal system to 'trust only guards'. Consequently, the position of prison guard is customarily handed down from one family member to the next. Garnering the role of a guard without the proper pedigree is analogous to winning the lottery. Accordingly, the seasoned 'Millhousers', as the guards proudly refer to themselves, will never fully accept Barr. He will always be an outsider. Only Barr's children can hope to gain acceptance one day, should one of them inherit a position in The Millhouse.

Tom shifts position, aims his camera and takes a photograph of the massive sculpture. He can take as many pictures as he wants. He is forbidden to take photos of the inmates without permission from prison management and any prisoner, who might find himself the subject of Tom's camera. Even within The Millhouse there are rules to protect the rights of the incarcerated. Barr watches the prisoners milling about at a distance. Although appearing to be indifferent, they are curious to know more about the reporter taking pictures of their sculpture. Tom moves to the front of the Walrus and takes another photo.

Moving in tandem with Tom, Barr constantly sweeps the area, looking for anomalies. He spots the warden walking toward them.

"Hi warden," greets Tom. "Thanks for letting me visit."

"Hi Tom. Call me Dan, short for Daniel. You know, Daniel and the lions. Last name is Gardner, if you need it for the piece you're writing."

"If you like, I can send ya a couple of pictures."

"That would be nice. Thanks. Are you getting everything you need? Is Bartholomew looking after you?"

"Everything's fine. This will make a great story. What can ya tell me about it?"

"It was a big chunk of papier-mâché when it first arrived. That was before I joined the ranks," says Dan. "There's an inmate inside by the name of Disposal-Man."

"What else can you tell me?" asks Tom, pulling out a pen and paper.

"It sat there untouched for the longest time. The guards didn't like it. It was a security issue because it blocked their view. One of the inmates approached me. He was an artist, a sculptor. He wanted to carve it into a walrus. He didn't say anything about a dancing walrus. Maybe he thought you had to show rather than say. He was right too; I wouldn't have understood. I guess that's what vision is about. Seeing what others don't see, making the invisible visible."

"What happened next?"

"There was a lot of discussion and paperwork, the usual kind of thing you find in an institution like this. It was a security nightmare. I'd come by from time to time to check on his progress. I enjoyed watching the transformation. When I realized that he was creating a dancing walrus, I asked him about it. He said he was honoring a potential in each of us."

"Can I meet the sculptor?"

"He's not here anymore. He finished his time. Hope things worked out for him. A few of the inmates seem to rise above their circumstance in some way. I think he was one of them."

"What's your take on the Walrus?"

"When I have time, I like to look at it, usually from up there," says Dan, pointing to the catwalk that circles the perimeter of the common area. "I don't usually come down here, even though the perspective is better. When you stand next to the sculpture, it has an immediacy, a presence that you don't find on the catwalk. There was a change in The Millhouse when the carving was finished. Many of the inmates like it. They say it's a work of art. The place is calmer. There aren't as many incidents now. A bunch of the inmates spend their time circling the piece, looking for things they haven't noticed before. A few of them study it and discuss what they see. A couple of them enrolled in an art history correspondence course offered by a university. Why not? Some of them have lots of time."

"Yes, I can see why they might do that," says Tom, looking more closely at the sculpture. "Here's an advertisement from a music store. It's offering introductory lessons with the purchase of a guitar or saxophone," Tom notes. "Hey, this looks like the anniversary edition of the Lickspittle. I remember working on that. There was a special insert," says Tom, getting excited about his discovery. "There were photos from the past sixty years. This is amazing! It's full of nuances, isn't it? You could look at this for a long time and still not see it all."

"Yes, that's true. And that advertisement inspired a couple of inmates to take up the guitar. And others..."

"Look! Here's a picture of a guy with binoculars. It's like he's looking back at the reader. I wonder what he's thinking. And look at the cars. Here's one with fins, and taillights that seem like rockets blasting off into space. It was the age of rocketry. People wanted to believe in technology and the future, the open road. And look at the faces of the people. The men are wearing the broad-brim hats that were common then. It was a different time, at least in terms of style."

"A few of the inmates talk about the music that the Walrus is dancing to," Dan resumes. "What music does it hear? A couple of them make the obvious choice, *I Am the Walrus*. A brave few say *Dance Me to the End of Love*."

"Why brave?"

"Look around you. What do you see? Those kinds of thoughts aren't readily shared in this environment. I've heard lots of good suggestions as to the music. Still others ask a different question. What is the Walrus' song? They believe that the song is unique, a song based on personal experiences. Occasionally, a discussion gets a little heated. The guards step in and cool things down when that happens. Usually the inmates look a little embarrassed. It goes against what The Dancing Walrus is saying and they know it, even if they can't put it into words. They've broken faith."

"And which way do you think it is?"

"I favor the idea that it's a self-composition."

"Why so?"

"Because…" Dan pauses, trying to put his thought into words. "Ever had a moment when you … You're surprised by an event that touches you in a way that you hadn't expected. You can't put it into words and maybe it isn't a song in the way we think of a song. It's different for each of us. And you hang onto the memory of that event because it goes to the core of who you are and the core of … of everything. That's maybe…" Dan is lost in thought. "It seems strange to be talking about this kind of experience in a correctional institution, or maybe it's not so strange. Why should this place be any different?"

"Anyone get hurt?" Tom asks, looking for a storyline.

"What?" asks Dan, looking a little distant.

"These discussions about the music, anyone get hurt? People are interested in who, what, where, when and why," Tom clarifies. "If I start describing things not easily explained, I'll lose a lot of eyeballs."

Dan looks confused. "Oh, you mean readers, eyeballs. Oh, I see. No, no one's been hurt. The inmates held a secret vote a few months ago about the music. They put the most popular suggestions on a ballot. Some refused to participate. They were the ones that thought the Walrus was hearing its own song, so you couldn't name it. I sanctioned the voting. It was an exercise in democracy. The inmates were responsible for the balloting. Things went a little sour though. Some of them became a little too competitive, each one wanting his choice to win. There were accusations of voting irregularities. In the end, they declared the results null and void. Too bad, or maybe not."

"Why maybe not?"

"Some said naming a song would impose a limitation on the meaning of the sculpture. They said it would be like

94

trying to nail jelly to the wall. Some things shouldn't be fixed and can't be fixed without a lot of effort and losing the meaning along the way. Maybe that's not the best analogy."

"What will happen to the sculpture?"

"One of the prisoners learned of a walrus kept in a sea aquarium in a subtropical climate," Dan adds, ignoring Tom's question. "He started a campaign to free the animal. He said it was unnatural to keep it in such a hot place, even though it had all the comforts of home. Turns out the walrus had lived in captivity a long time and wasn't likely to survive in the Arctic Ocean. Many of the inmates were disappointed, feeling that something important was lost. I know what they mean. Things don't always work out. A few continued to advocate on behalf of the animal. They thought that it was better to die free than live in captivity."

"What do you think about freeing it?"

Dan hesitates. "I don't know. It probably would have declined the offer for that kind of freedom. Maybe the walrus already thought it was free: free from predators, free from having to hunt for clams. Things were good."

"A pragmatic walrus?"

"Sure, why not? The will to continue is the most powerful force in all of nature. I see it all the time in here. Why should the walrus be any different? Maybe I'm transferring my thoughts and feelings onto the animal."

"What will happen to the sculpture?" asks Tom, repeating his earlier question.

"He's got another year or so to run, Disposal-Man that is. Then we'll let him out for good behavior, not that he could do anything else. We'll cut open the sculpture and let him go. Shame about that, I mean taking it apart. We can't keep Disposal-Man. He'll have served his sentence. We'll try to integrate him into society."

Without warning, the sculpture vibrates for a minute and then stops.

"What was that?" Tom asks.

"Oh, it's okay. We're not sure what he's doing in there. Whatever it is, it seems harmless. He's never tried to break out. I don't think he can."

Dan looks at his watch. "It's time for you to go. It'll soon be dinner time. The men get anxious if they can't follow the routine. You get used to it."

Mummers 'llowed In?

Joe cuts the outboard engine. It sputters and stops. The wooden dory glides forward, urged on by its inertia. The boat encounters the gentle roll of a sluggish wave where the Labrador Current and the Gulf Stream mix. The bow of the dory rises gently and casually drops.

'Slap,' says the dory's hull, finding the trough of the wave.

Wrapped in a cold fog, Joe shudders. He listens for the sound of the waves mounting the pebbled shoreline that hugs the nearby cliff. The cliff stands outside the harbor to Away Home Bay, an isolated outport inhabited by two-hundred souls, give or take a few.

Joe is from away. You were considered from away if your family lineage didn't extend at least three generations back into the community. Most of the villagers can trace their ancestry to Europeans, who arrived over three-hundred years ago.

Joe was drawn to the outport last summer with the rumor of work on a seiner based in Away Home Bay. Since his arrival, he has managed to scrape out a living as a flunky on the boat.

'Shshshshshshsh,' says a wave breaking against the shore.

'Clickety-click,' answer the pebbles, tumbling in the wash of the wave.

"'Bout a gunshot away," Joe mutters, gauging his distance from the shoreline by the sound of the waves.

The dory halts, having lost its momentum against the oncoming waves.

Intermittently, Atlantic puffins from a nearby colony, skimming above the water, dart out of the fog. Joe can hear the whisper of their wings beating against the air. They veer sharply away from the dory and disappear into the fog.

The fishing isn't very good since the decline of the fish stocks. In the off season, Joe translates for tourists the often-quirky language of the village residents. Joe, in his short time in the outport, has learned a smattering of phrases common to the residents. After an early encounter with an 'old feller' and onetime fisherman, Jeremiah, Joe realized that, if he wanted to fit in, he needed to learn at least the bare bones of the lingo.

"Do ya come from away?" asked Jeremiah, whom Joe met on the government wharf. "Ya must be from away. Are ya a flatlander? Ya looks like ya've been drugged through a knothole," Jeremiah observed, examining Joe's nor'wester hair, bear-ragged beard, moose-antlered shirt and pants, and holed-out piss-quicks. "'Ave ya been runned over by a moose, b'y?" Jeremiah queried good-naturedly. He wondered if Joe had recently arrived from one of the logging camps in the interior. "You're clear o' the mooseflies now. I'll says d'at much."

At the time of his encounter with Jeremiah, Joe had been in the village less than a day, having spent several days reaching it. He was hungry and low on cash.

"I'm looking for work. I heard one of the seiners might need a crew member," responded Joe. "Do ya know if anyone is looking for crew?"

"There's the Johnny Magorey. Ya knows the Johnny Magorey, does ya?" asked Jeremiah with a smile. "I'll tells ya a story 'bout Johnny Magorey. Shall I begin? And now I'm done." He winks mischievously at Joe. "Does ya know 'er?" He asked playfully. "She's da only one left 'ere now.

She goes after mackerel, 'erring and such when d'eys runnin' and da fish plants runnin' up in Trunk 'ole 'arbour. Can ya runs a skiff? Ya needs to see William. 'E's da skipper. D'ey calls 'im Skippy. Lives up da hill in da green and blue 'ouse," offered Jeremiah, nodding vaguely toward the far end of the village. "Used to be 'is mudder's. She's passed now. She lived on a long stretch after 'er 'usband, Skippy's fat'er."

"Which street is that?"

"Does ya know da Riley's 'ouse? D'eir son's away on one o' da rigs. I knows 'im since 'e was a gaffer. Got 'is ticket now, diesel mechanic. Went away to get it. 'E's a townie now. Gets 'ome at Christmas time maybe, if 'e's not on da rig. Does ya knows 'im? Name's Michael. We calls 'im Nokes. 'E's a sharp one. Nothin' simple 'bout 'im. 'E's a good catch. Married one o' da Connor sisters, Rebecca. D'ere's da t'ree o' d'em, Rebecca, Rachel and Ruth. Rebecca, we calls Puddin'. I believes. D'en d'ere's Apple, d'at's Rachel, and Sally, d'at's Ruth. Don't knows why we calls 'er d'at. Maybe after 'er aunt downs d'ere in 'oly Rude Bay. Ya can ask d'em yourself. Apple's 'itched. Sally's not. She'd be a good catch for ya. Though ya'd 'ave to smarten yourself up some. Da Connors lives two doors up from the Rileys in da red 'ouse. D'eys not far off, a stone's t'row from William's place."

Joe stared blankly, waiting quietly in hopes of more information that would help pinpoint William's house.

"'E's not d'ere now. Waits till 'e comes back."

"How soon will he be back?" Joe abandoned any hope of learning the location of the William's place from Jeremiah.

"'Bout duckish, I believes. I don't knows ya," said Jeremiah, returning to his earlier thread. "And I don't' t'ink you're a townie, are ya? Where she longs at?"

"Longs at?"

"Where ya from? Where's your talk from? You're not one o' da tourist types I sees 'ere 'bout, lookin' for da whales."

In recent years, the community had become one of the hotspots along the coast for tourists interested in watching whales migrate along the coastline. A few of the locals supplement their income by ferrying tourists into deep water in search of Humpback, Fin, Sperm, and other denizens of the North Atlantic.

Infrequently, a tourist would long for the perceived simpler life of the outport, not seeing the hard struggle that such a life could bring with it. There were dreams of running a bed and breakfast. Usually these tourists didn't last more than a few seasons when confronted with the reality. They were soon headed back to the environs they knew best, which didn't seem like such a bad place after all.

"Who owns ya?" asked Jeremiah. The question was his way of asking Joe the names of his parents.

"Owns me?"

"You're like a fish out o' water," Jeremiah observed.

Despite his best efforts, Joe has never fully mastered the patois practiced by the residents of Away Home Bay. His limited vernacular is more a mixture of the many idioms encountered in several outports.

Coming forward in the dory, Joe grabs the anchor and lowers it over the side. The anchor chain plays out. The links drub lightly against the gunwale.

'Grumble, grumble,' complains the chain, until the anchor finds bottom.

Joe ties off the chain. Then, lowering a line into the water, he jigs for cod.

After an hour of jigging, two small cod lie in the bottom of the dory. The fishing isn't good. Joe persists in hopes of a better bounty.

'Scrough, scrough,' coughs the shore in protest, as pebbles scrunch and scurry out from under the shoes of someone walking the strand.

Joe listens carefully.

'Scrough, scrough…' repeats the shore in unison with the hiker's purposeful steps.

The newcomer stops when he reaches the end of the short stretch of beach. The cliff impedes further advancement.

Must be a tourist, Joe surmises.

Sometimes they find their way down to the shore at the base of the cliff. Usually they're looking for the cliff top that affords a panoramic view of the water and, on occasion, the sighting of a passing whale. Today the fog blocks any semblance of a view, including that of Joe.

'Scrough, scrough, scrough…' says the shore. 'Scrough!' The sound comes to a halt.

The walker seems perplexed, unsure of what to do.

"Is ya lookin' for da whales?" shouts Joe, assuming a lost whale watcher, or perhaps someone scouting the village as a potential site for an upscale resort.

From time to time, there's talk that a few of the townies might build a retreat, consisting of a dozen, high-end cottages for the well-heeled tourists. Visitors would come for a respite from the city: Toronto, New York, London, or maybe even as far away as Tokyo.

In addition to the ocean and the awe-inspiring vistas, the villagers are considered a drawing card for their genuine nature. One of the would-be promoters of a resort produced a brochure that espoused the 'undeniable authenticity' of the residents. What did 'authenticity' mean, Joe wondered? The villagers have a 'genetic predisposition' to hospitality according to the leaflet. It went on to point out that the villagers' sociability makes each of them a natural concierge. Joe had to look up the word concierge. He discovered it means someone who helps others. He decided this was true. How could you be otherwise in an outport where everyone depended on everyone else? The brochure talked of 'leveraging the community's economic and cultural resilience' and 'revitalizing the community'. There would be an artisan's guild for crafts, along with walking guides, storytellers and more. The document concluded with these words: 'The alignment of the people, their purpose, and the place make a natural harbor for weary city dwellers looking for a break from the daily grind of big-city life.'

"Steers back t'other way. Takes the path that bears right when ya comes to 'er."

'Scrough?'

"Where's ya at?" asks Joe. There's no response. "Stays where you're at and I'll comes where you're to." He begins pulling in his line. "I'll be d'ere d'rackley."

"I'm looking for someone," says a voice emerging from the fog. "Are you from Away Home Bay?" The voice carries strangely, seeming to originate from everywhere.

"Who? I knows most o' d'em."

"Do you know Borj?"

"Don't knows 'im. Does he come from away?"

"Away?"

"Not from 'ere, Away Home Bay. Is 'e a flatlander or maybe a townie?"

"Yeah, he's from," the voice searches for the word, "away." The word sounds strange and tentative. "What's your name?"

"Guffy."

"Is that your last name or your first name?"

"Guffy, d'at's what d'ey calls me."

'Scrough, scrough.'

"Does ya mean who owns me?"

"Who owns me?"

"Yeah, me parents."

"What's your last name?"

"Mummer."

"Mummer?"

"Yeah, like the ones d'at comes to your 'ouse after Christmas."

The dory rises on a wave and dips into the trough.

'Slap,' the dory says helpfully. There's no response from shore.

"Mummers 'llowed in?" Joe offers. He disguises his voice in the tradition of a mummer. "Does ya understands mummer?" he shouts, uncertain if 'mummers 'llowed in' got lost somewhere between the boat and shore.

"What's your first name again?"

"Joe, Joe Mummer," he answers, hauling in the anchor.

"I thought you said your name was Guffy."

"It's Joe. D'ey calls me Guffy 'cause I'm like da fish."

"Like the fish?"

"Ya knows. Da guffy's a fish, a scavenger. Only I hunts for work."

There is no response to this morsel of information.

Joe moves to the stern of the boat where he yanks on the engine pull cord. The motor sputters, pops and grumbles to life. He shifts it into forward and cautiously points the dory toward shore. Straining, he peers into the fog. Slowly, the figure of a man emerges. He's wearing a black hoodie. Slung over his shoulder is a leather satchel. Joe cuts the engine. The boat glides forward. The prow rides up gently, kissing the gravel shore.

"How's she cuttin' d'ere b'y?" Joe offers by way of a greeting. "I'll takes ya in." He peers at the outsider, trying to see the face half hidden by the hoodie. "What's your name?" Joe asks, avoiding the local speech in order to be understood.

"Monk-Man, they call me Monk-Man."

What kind a name is d'at? Joe wonders.

"Don't knows d'at one. Well, youse from away." Joe observes with a smile. "Gives 'er a push and jumps in."

Monk pushes off, clambers into the prow and plunks himself down on the forward thwart, keeping his back to Joe. Joe nudges the engine into gear and points the dory toward the harbor. Monk turns briefly to look at Joe, who smiles in response. He's too busy to talk. Navigating the short trip takes concentration.

"Keeps an eye out so's we don't 'its nothin'."

Clearing the entrance, Joe steers the dory toward a wooden dock erected by one of the local fishermen.

"Jumps out and ties 'er off," says Joe.

Monk grabs a rope. He scrambles onto the dock and ties off the bow. Joe tosses him the rope for the stern, which Monk also secures.

"Is there some place we can talk?" asks Monk, once Joe has shifted himself to the dock.

"Ya looks like ya been eatin' da putty outta da windows. We can 'ave a mug up at me place," Joe offers good naturedly. He's unable or unwilling to escape completely the village lingo. "We can hikes up d'ere," he appends, with a vague nod in the direction of the village, "after I clean d'ese." He holds up his two fish.

With practiced hands, Joe expertly cleans his catch. Monk looks on, studying Joe.

"How long have you been doing that?"

"Doin' what?"

"Cleaning fish."

"A minute, I guess."

"No, I mean have you been doing that all your life?"

"Don't knows. Long as I cans remember."

No more words are spoken and Joe is soon finished.

They climb the hill to the green-blue house belonging to the skipper of the Johnny Magorey. Joe bartered his services as a deckhand in return for a share in the proceeds from the ship's catch, and for two small rooms: a simple kitchen and a bedroom. To Monk's sense of time, the short walk takes hours, owing to Joe's propensity to stop and chat with villagers met along the way.

104

What's After Happenin' Now?

Joe cuts two thick slices of bread. He retrieves butter, jam and a small carton of milk and sets them on the kitchen table. Monk watches as his host prepares tea. Joe joins Monk at the table.

"What does ya says d'ey calls 'im?"

"Borj."

"D'at's a strange one. Just Borj?"

"Yeah, Borj."

Joe pours tea, while turning the name over in his head. He adds a splotch of milk to his mug and slides the milk across the table.

"'Elps yourself."

Monk takes a slice of bread and spreads on butter and jam. He takes a bite, relishing the simple meal, not having eaten since yesterday. A look of satisfaction crosses his face. He takes a sip of tea.

Joe watches his every move with curiosity.

"I knows most o' da b'ys 'ere."

"That's okay. I think I found him."

"Was it one o' da b'ys we passed on da way 'ere? I knows d'em. None of d'em goes by d'at name."

Monk reaches for his satchel, removes a manila envelope and pulls out a picture of three men standing beside an old black car. The picture is recent. He slides it across the table.

"Do you know any of these people?"

"I don't knows d'em. Who are d'ey? Is one o' d'em Borj?" Joe has the uneasy feeling that he's in a Johnny Magorey verse.

"They're people Borj knew."

"What does he looks like?"

"He looks like you," Monk answers calmly. He watches for a response. "Ya were hard to track down. It's taken me months to find you after learning 'bout your run in with a super villain. There were a lot of blind alleys."

"Lord t'underin' Jesus! Does ya not t'ink I knows who I am?"

"The guy on the right and left in the picture are Slash and Razor." Monk persists, ignoring Joe's protest.

"Which is which d'en?"

"You knew them when they were called Stapes and P-Cut. The guy on the left is Stapes and the one on the right is P-Cut. They were superheroes. They fought super villains. You did too. You lived in the city of Lore. The four of us worked out of the same office for a while."

"Your thwarts are too far aft."

"Professionally they were known as Stapler-Man and Paper-Cut-Man. Their designation was T3. You had the same designation, but never mind that. What's important is that you're not who you think you are."

"Go 'way! You're full o' shit and up a quart!" exclaims Joe, finding comfort in the patois. "I'm sure I wouldn't be disrememberin' any o' d'is if it were true."

"We'll come to that. The disremembering, I mean."

"And what was your name? Did ya have two names like everyone else in d'is 'ere yarn you're spinnin'?"

"Before I was Monk-Man, I was Hothead-Man, a villain, and not a very good one."

"Ya was what?"

"I was a villain."

"Oh, I sees," Joe says suspiciously. "And what's a Hothead-Man."

"I tried to influence people for my own ends."

106

"And how did ya do d'at?"

"I found I could make people's heads hot. I wasn't very good at it. I realized I was wrong for the part, so I changed sides. Later I figured out I needed to be on my side. Does that make sense?"

"Ya needs 'elp. Was it William d'at put ya up to d'is? He likes his Johnny Magorey. Does ya knows William? Is ya related?"

"Here, look. I found this in what was left of your scooter." Monk rummages in his satchel. He pulls out an item and lays it on the table as though playing a trump card.

"What's d'is?" asks Joe, ignoring the question surrounding the likelihood of Joe ever owning a scooter and what terrible accident befell the machine.

"It's the ID badge that Cornelius gave you when you worked at the agency."

"What agency was d'at? And who's Cornelius?"

Joe looks at the picture on the battered badge. He turns it over in his hand, examining both sides. Chunks of it are missing and the overlying stamp impressions hide most of what remains of the face. Still, Joe finds something troubling in the photo.

"You're makin' d'is up! D'is could be anyone!" Joe licks a couple of his fingers and rubs the badge, trying to remove the dirt and grease.

"No, it's true," Monk persists. "You worked for NPA."

"I'm t'understruck! What's d'at?"

"The National Protection Agency. The guy in the middle of the picture is Cornelius. He's Identity-Man. There was a breach in security. He managed to get a job at the agency. No one knew who he was. He's very good at hiding his true self. He can move freely about in society without being recognized."

"Ya don't really expects me to believe all d'is, does ya? You're good for yarnin'. I'll give ya d'at," Joe scoffs.

"Identity-Man is a super villain, the nemesis of you and everyone. He assigns new identities to people when it suits him. That's why you're..." Monk pauses, searching for the right word, "disremembering. He does it for his own purposes. He tells them who they are and feeds them false dreams and hopes that they buy into. It's his propaganda. It's his way of getting people to do what he wants for his own ends. They start fighting for the wrong things because they don't know who they really are."

"And why would he be doin' d'at? I knows who I am, like most."

"I don't know why," says Monk. "I know he has a global plan and global influence. Maybe you threatened his plan, so he wanted you out of the way. That's all I know."

"Next, you'll be tellin' me d'ere's aliens too," scoffs Joe.

"There is one. His name is Disposal-Man. The two of us used papier-mâché to capture him in an old silo at The Flour Mill in Lore."

"You're talkin' janny," Joe counters. "We did what? Why would we be doin' d'at?" Joe's head is beginning to swirl with talk of all these strange names, faces and events.

"Look, I can prove it," Monk entreats. He pulls out a tattered newspaper clipping and hands it to Joe. The article is from the Lickspittle Free Press. Monk takes a sip of his tea followed by a bite out of his bread while Joe reads.

"It says 'ere d'ey let him out o' the Millhouse Correctional Institution. And anyway, d'is doesn't ties me to any o' d'is. It says some guy named Borj, who could be anyone, and some guy named Monk-Man captured d'is guy. And ya says youse Monk-Man. How does I know you're who ya says ya are? And what's d'is got to do with me?" Looking up from the newspaper clipping, he squints at Monk, expecting a straight answer. "'As ya been in the bush too long?" he asks skeptically. "I can sees you're strapped. I brings ya into me 'ouse and I feeds ya. And ya says I don't knows who I am. How can d'at be? Who put ya up to d'is? Don't tries to fool me."

"It's all true," pleads Monk. "You had a run in with Identity-Man. You didn't know who he was. He gave you a new identity, the one you have now, d'is one," answers Monk, who is unconsciously beginning to pick up the lingo.

"You're draggin' da roads. Go on 'ome. Your mudder's got 'lassy buns," says Joe, slathering on the local language to reassure himself who he is and that he belongs in Away Home Bay. "I t'inks youse da villain! You're tryin' to tells me I'm not who I am."

"I know it's a lot to..."

"Away wich ya!" Joe demands with a sweeping gesture of his hand toward the door.

Monk stands up reluctantly.

"I've got one more thing to show you before I go. I want you to reads d'is." He pulls a tattered notebook from his satchel. He offers it to his host.

"What's d'is?" Joe makes no effort to accept it.

"It's a journal. You wrote it," says Monk, laying it on the table. He walks to the door where he turns to look at Joe, who has his back to Monk. "Maybe it'll helps you to remember." He steps outside and closes the door.

'Click,' says the door.

With disbelieving eyes, Joe gazes at the closed notebook.

"What's after happenin' now?" asks the astounded Joe. He sips his tea in silence.

Mind of a Squid

Joe finishes his tea and bread, and washes up. Finally, unable to resist, he picks up the notebook, trying to weigh the import of its pages. He flips through it, expecting to find blank pages: a prop intended to bolster the elaborate tall tale perpetrated by one of the villagers. To his amazement, he finds it's crammed with entries.

"Not even old William would go to d'is trouble to 'ave 'is fun," Joe notes. "D'ats da truth o' 'er."

A newspaper clipping falls to the floor. Joe picks it up. The article has a grainy picture with a caption, 'Borj receives key to Lore'. He takes in the image of the clean-shaven Borj and pulls reflectively on his beard. A moment of astonishment and then doubt flashes across his face.

"Come on now!" he mumbles in disbelief. "She can't be."

He opens the journal.

Oct 5
Disposal-Man.
Almost blended into the mix by his industrial-strength blender! Stopped him with Monk's help. Would've been easier with my sax and less collateral damage. Don't know about Disposal-Man. Where did he come from? What was he after? How do you read a machine? Monk and I had a long walk home. Watched the sun come up. Felt good to be alive!
Don't expect to see Monk again. He's looking for something, not sure he knows what.

Reading long into the night, Joe tries to pry a glimpse into the writer's character. In the morning, he awakes slumped over the kitchen table. He reads the last entry. There's no date.

Lore is deserted except for The Millhouse and a few stragglers.
Why stay?

Joe examines the picture on the temporary badge. He struggles to piece together the hidden features of a clean-shaven face. One eye is obliterated by the impression from a stamp. The other eye peers back. The color is right.

"Ya don't knows your own face, does ya?" Joe observes.

Opening a cupboard drawer, he retrieves a knife and methodically hacks away his beard. He runs his hands roughly through his hair to approximate the hairstyle in the pictures. He looks in the mirror over the kitchen sink to examine the result.

"'As ya been t'rough a wood chipper? Not d'at youse much to see at da best o' times. Ya got a face d'at only a mudder could love."

He places a wash basin in the sink and fills it with hot water. He lathers up and removes the remnants of his beard with a razor. Joe diligently examines every curve of his face, as though seeing it for the first time. Alternately, he holds the dilapidated badge and the newspaper clipping beside the mirror, comparing them to his face. Uncertain, he wipes away the remaining lather and assesses once more.

"Ya got da mind of a squid," he allows, feeling exasperated. "Ya don't knows if youse comin' or goin'. What's da answer?"

Do What Ya 'As To

'Knock, knock, knock' says the front door of the Connor house.

Joe waits. There's no response.

"Come on wich ya Sally. Where's ya at?" he complains.

'Knock, knock, knock'

Joe starts to walk away.

'Clclatch' says the door.

"Hi Joe," says Sally with a welcoming smile. "How is ya? What's happened to ya? Ya've shaved off your beard. Ya looks nice. Would ya likes to come in? I was goin' to 'ave a cup o' tea. Would ya likes one?" she coaxes, pleased to see Joe.

"Yes, I'd likes d'at," he answers, looking troubled.

"Well comes in d'en."

"Da fish plant's runnin'," Sally continues, having made her way to the kitchen with Joe in tow. "Has ya been out on da Johnny Magorey?"

Looking preoccupied, Joe says nothing. He sits down at the kitchen table.

"Was ya at da dance last night? I didn't sees ya," Sally notes, sounding a little disappointed, and puzzled by his unresponsiveness. She places a plate of cookies on the table. "Helps yourself. I just took d'em out o' da oven. It's not likes ya to miss da dance. Was ya sick?"

"No, I was readin' a book, a journal." He reaches mechanically for a cookie and takes a bite. "Ya makes da best 'lassy buns," he adds, smiling and warming a little to the conversation.

"Oh, a journal," echoes Sally. "I didn't knows d'at ya likes to read. Where did ya get da journal?"

"'E said 'is name is Monk-Man of all t'ings," responds Joe in disbelief. "'E gave it to me. 'E said 'e was from Lore and d'at I used to know 'im."

"Lore, d'ats a long way." Hiding a sinking feeling, she finds a chair, pours tea and places a cup in front of Joe. "D'ere's sugar and milk too." She smiles, masking an unwanted premonition.

Joe pours milk into his tea and takes a sip. "'E said I wrote it." He pulls out the hitherto hidden notebook from his jacket and places it on the table. "It's a good yarn. I'll give 'er d'at. I t'ought it was one o' William's tricks. Now I don't knows what to t'ink." He pulls the newspaper clipping from the journal and slides it across the table to Sally. "I needs someone d'at will treat me honest. Would ya 'ave a look at d'is? What does ya t'ink? Is d'at me?"

Sally picks up the picture, uncertain if she wants to turn into the headwind. She studies the picture for a moment. "I don't knows." She pulls a magnifying glass from a drawer and examines the likeness carefully. "It's 'ard to tell. It's a poor picture," she decides, satisfied that she has given an honest answer. "It could be you, d'en it could be lots o' folks too," she adds, to reinforce her conclusion. "Does ya not know yourself? Youse from away. Where's away?"

"I always t'ought I was from 'ere abouts, maybe a townie. I don't knows meself."

"Can I reads some o' da journal?" asks Sally, reaching for it without waiting for an answer. She flips through the pages. She stops randomly, reads an entry and then flips to another one. She listens for Joe's voice in the words and the spaces between the words. She suddenly stops. The notebook lies open on the table. She crosses her arms defensively, not fully convinced by what she's heard.

"I can't tells if d'is is you. Maybe it is and maybe it isn't. You're a mystery," Sally observes. "Who owns ya d'en?" In need of an answer for his sake and her own, she looks with trepidation at him. "Ya must knows d'at," she asserts, suppressing her anger at Joe for not knowing and at herself for caring too much for him that knowing didn't matter. "'As ya done somethin'? Is d'at whys you're 'ere in da Bay? Is ya hidin' out?" she questions. "Youse a good man," she adds, wanting to take back her question because she knows it's not in him. "I knows d'at. We all does."

"Mummers 'llowed in," he answers weakly, feeling overwhelmed. Nothing more comes to mind.

"Ya needs to know who ya are," Sally replies resolutely, trying to stay firm for both.

Joe pulls the temp badge from his coat. He hands it to her. She looks at the mangled one-eyed badge. A lump forms in her throat. She recognizes the truth in that single eye that looks at her. Feeling defeated by the headwind blowing against her, she swallows hard and turns to, unable to hold against the gale.

"Who's d'is d'en?" She places the badge carefully on the table and pushes it away, not wanting its truth near her.

"Borj, 'is name is Borj." Joe looks down at his boots, shuffling them uncomfortably on the worn linoleum floor. He realizes now that he's put Sally in a difficult spot and is ashamed for doing so, while recognizing that he must have an answer.

"Oh Joe," she manages to say, feeling besieged. She wants to deny what she can see, but she can't ignore the truth, if she is to remain true to herself and Joe. "What can I say? It's you. D'ere's no doubt in me mind. Ya knows it too, don't ya?"

Joe nods his head. "I needed to 'ear it from someone else: you. I didn't wants to believe it."

"Why did it 'as to be me that ya comes to?"

"Youse an anchor."

"Joe, who is ya?" Sally asks, looking him straight in the eye with the tears welling up. "Ya 'as to be true to who ya is. And only you can answers d'at one. D'ere's no one else d'at can do it for ya, only you." A tear trickles down her cheek. She quickly wipes it away.

"I needs to find out. I needs to go to Lore. Da answer's d'ere."

"Do what ya 'as to."

Easy to Loose

About a week later and having said his goodbyes, Joe looks at the receding Away Home Bay from the deck of the supply ship, 'Running the Goat'. Slung over his shoulder, he carries a worn knapsack with his few possessions, including the journal.

'Thrum, thrum' sings the ship's engine. The propeller screw with each turn pushes the vessel a little closer to the mouth of the harbor. On the pier and growing smaller, is Jeremiah. He was Joe's last encounter with one of the locals.

"How's she cuttin' 'er b'y?" asked Jeremiah, who spied Joe waiting to board.

"She's good."

"Is ya leavin' us?"

"Yeah, I don't belongs 'ere. I'm from away."

"Where's ya to?"

"Lore."

"Lore. Don't knows d'at one. Don't be disrememberin'," warned Jeremiah. "We's got to keep the lingo. She's easy to loose."

Joe smiled feebly as he stepped onto the gangplank.

"And don't pick the red ones, d'eys green." Jeremiah added with a grin.

Several great black-backed gulls circle above the Puffin colony. Returning puffins, having foraged for fish at sea, do their best to avoid the gulls. Joe watches the cliff slowly sink below the horizon. He can feel Away Home Bay and its residents slipping away.

After stops at numerous villages, the ship docks at its home port, Accidental Rapture, where Joe catches a train. With each clickety-clack of the train wheels, the speech of the outports falls away.

BQT

Joe hunkers down behind the skeletal remains of a truck. He peers warily at the office building on the opposite side of the street. Seemingly impervious to time, the edifice is untouched by the surrounding decay that eats away at Lore. The owner, wanting to impress his clients and to inspire his work force to greater monetary success, commissioned a building that would make Hermes, the god of commerce, proud. In a time before steel-framed structures wrapped in glass, the three-storey monolith was pronounced an architectural marvel; a masterpiece of ashlars, white-marble facade, three-bay pediments, a plethora of supporting columns adorned with Corinthian and Doric porticoes, balustraded parapets, and a copper roof that has acquired a rich patina denoting age and former success. Attesting to the brevity of success, a large 'For Sale' sign, strung between several of the support columns, flaps sluggishly in the wind.

With each passing year and mounting commercial achievements, the facility grew. Squatting behind the office building, the owner's vision of an industrial Xanadu expanded into a warren of structures of various shapes and sizes. Eventually the massive construction dominated several city blocks. Where intervening streets threatened to impede the efficient flow of goods and personnel, the owner erected enclosed, overhead walkways to provide conduits between buildings. In its youth, the facility was a mechanized marvel that garnered loads of awards from

118

associations that keenly embraced modern manufacturing methods. The complex was a utilitarian world of wonders.

Excited employees got into the act too. In the interest of saving time, workers reduced words and phrases to initialism and acronyms. For example, workers referred to the company, Buzz Quick Time Co., as BQT. Minimalism, having languished for decades in the art movement before BQT breathed life into it, became the catch word for a dynamic and evolving industry.

Shortening words and phrases became so prevalent within the company that each FQ (Fiscal Quarter) BQT produced an OG (Official Glossary) of terms for new employees to learn. The goal was to get the newbies (NBs) up to BQT speed quickly. There was no time to waste. NBs memorized the terms in their spare time. The OG was forever changing when workers discovered new ways to abbreviate anything and everything in the interest of going faster, no matter what the task. Speed was the holiest of holies in this dynamic world. And leading the way was the juggernaut BQT, which ruthlessly bulldozed old manufacturing methods into rubble, while forging a new path in up-to-the-minute processes.

At BQT's zenith, a department of twenty people was tasked with maintaining the OG in the interest of efficiency. The department was officially known as CtC (Cut the Crap). Within CtC was a special group, the CPers (Crap Police). Their job was to wander incognito throughout the facility and seek out employees whose BQT speak was not buzz-quick enough. A first offense meant a letter of reprimand known as a LoCR (Letter of Crap Reprimand). A LoCR would severely cripple an employee's potential for advancement within the organization. A second LoCR would likely lead to dismissal: NMCfU (No More Crap from You). The CtC department was so important to the welfare of BQT that a committee, LNTB (Leave No Turds Behind), was struck to oversee the work of CtC. LNTB's role was to ensure that

CtC remained true to its minimalist roots. LNTB reported to the CMO (Chief Minimalist Officer), who reported directly to the CEO.

No expense was spared. Linguists from the nearby university were brought in to study and offer advice on points of grammar in this evolving language. Erudite efficiency experts wrote scholarly papers extolling the value of this new, lean lingo, the minimalism of the future. BQT's notoriety propelled the company to the top, making it *the* GTL (Global Thought Leader) by which all other companies were judged in the ethereal realm of business communication.

Some employees became so wedded to BQT that they spoke only BQT to their SnC (Spouses and Children). Whole families and later entire neighborhoods began speaking BQT. One industrious employee created and privately published his own glossary called *BQT at Home* (BQTaH). BQTaH was a big hit. The glossary introduced new DTs (Domestic Terms) to BQT EnFs (Employees and Families). Eventually DTs became part of the BQT vernacular at work in a CcP (Cross-culture Pollination) with each culture influencing the other. At one time, the SB (ScuttleButt) in the office was that BQT would BtR (Buy the Rights) to the DV (Domestic Version) and enhance it in order to BIFem (Better Integrate Family Members) into the BQT family and BQT's ST (Speak Think). Those were head-buzzing, body-tingling days of never-ending CcP.

The incessant drone of terms was amazing. ST spread at a feverish pitch throughout Lore and beyond its confines. Like an epidemic, ST could not be contained. People were stupefied by the speed and efficiency at which it spread. It was as though Hermes himself was championing its expansion at a velocity faster than thought.

Alas, progress in the golden age of commerce is unrelenting in its frantic flight. The fortunes of BQT declined. Fortunately, ST (Speak Think) had by this time taken on a life of its own, growing and evolving globally,

120

thriving in other corporate cultures. Linguists and efficiency experts, having picked clean the bones of ST, abandoned BQT in favor of the richer Elysian Fields offered by the new TLs (Thought Leaders) in the field of ST. On the world stage, BQT's ST transformed into BiCS (Best in Class Speak) where it continues to FnE (Flourish and Evolve).

Now ST is an almost lost language. Only a few dozen former employees speak and understand it. In the golden age of commerce, there's NoMoHo (No Mourning or Honoring) the giants on whose shoulders the new world builds. The ex-workers understand this unforgiving sentiment. Regarding their lost-tribe status, and in keeping with the harsh judgment inculcated by ST, they respond with indifference, 'W'sYerP?' (What's Your Point?), or sometimes the more plain-spoken ToSh (Tough Shit). Both terms gained prevalence in the last few years that preceded the demise of BQT. In the final months, BQT employees, who by this time had been kicked around the block untold times, coined one last term for the BQT lexicon: WS (We're Screwed), which was never officially recognized, not having found credence in the OG (Official Glossary). There was no one left to add WS to the OG, which was abandoned several years prior. ToSh.

During the death throes of BQT, the owner attempted to sell the building. To do this, he wanted to showcase the pinnacle of his architectural achievement: the marvelous front-office facade. BQT asked the one surviving BQT Pho (Photographer) to create a portfolio of pictures that the real-estate agent engaged by BQT could use to bolster the sale of the facility. The Pho had for several decades recorded the beehive of manufacturing activity. He knew many of the workers. Not surprisingly, the Pho chose to photograph the front of the complex during a shift change by the anemically few workers who scurried in all directions after another grinding day of WS. Overcoming his own sense of WS, the Pho created an historical record representative of the last days of BQT. The Pho, like many of the employees, could see the inevitable end with new industries taking root in distant cities, like New Grubbeemitts, and quickly growing to become the new leviathans on the world stage of business.

The real-estate agent insisted that the Pho reshoot the front of the building without the presence of a bunch of workers dragging their tired asses. The Pho refused, negating the ToSh attitude and ending his long career at BQT, NMCfU (No More Crap from You). An outside Pho was brought in to redo the job. The few stragglers who appeared in the reshot photos were digitally erased.

To aid in the transition during BQT's and Lore's precipitous decline, the Lickspittle Free Press ran articles about looking for work. At first the Lickspittle featured articles about the honey bees' proclivity to look for new food sources when known resources fell into decline. Later the articles were more direct, extolling the ever-expanding career opportunities trumpeted by the new global order in cities like New Grubbeemitts.

Nervously, Joe sprints by a derelict bus. He squats behind a rusting car sitting on its roof. His new position affords him a good view of the employees' entrance where a door gapes open.

He peers apprehensively. Someone has kept the area around the entrance clear of the usual street clutter. There's nowhere to hide. Joe ratchets his body into a compressed spring, readying himself for a sprint to the door.

"Wouldn't do that," says a voice behind him.

Joe spins 180 degrees. His heart quickens. A man hides in the shadow of a nearby doorway.

"Do what?" responds Joe, checking his surprise.

"Do what you're thinking of doing. And keep your voice down. Ya want to give yourself away? It's not safe. See those cameras? They'll see ya."

Joe turns and examines the cameras mounted on the office edifice. The cameras look to be in rough condition. "Do they still work?"

"Yeah, they work. Every now and then ya see one of them move, if you're patient."

"I've been watching the place for the last hour," Joe whispers, turning to the entranceway behind him. "I'm looking for someone. Is there anyone inside?"

"They're in there." The voice has moved a few doors down to another shadowy entryway. "It doesn't pay to stay too long in one place. Ya should move."

Joe hesitates. He runs toward the voice and leaps into the darkness. He waits for his eyes to adjust. He can make out the shape of a man standing in the corner.

"Now you're getting the idea. You'll be okay here for a couple of minutes. Don't get overconfident, worst thing ya can do. That's what they want. Ya start making mistakes and then..."

"Ya sound familiar. Do I know you?"

"Don't think so."

"What's your name?"

"You're not from around here, are ya?" says the shadow man, examining Joe. "Ya can't be one of Cornelius' gang. Sometimes they like to pose, look like a Strag."

"Strag?"

"Straggler. They try to draw ya out. If they catch ya, they'll send ya to Pawsoff. Kind of like a roundup. There's a labor shortage over there. They caught one of the holdouts last month. Haven't seen him since."

"How do ya know all this?"

"Watch and learn. For instance, they don't like people poking around here," he adds, lightly tapping Joe on the shoulder for emphasis.

Startled, Joe takes a step back.

"Chillax bud. Not going to hurt ya. Don't be so jumpy. Guess you're like the rest, not like Cornelius and his gang. They're a cocky bunch."

"Who's he?" asks Joe, hoping to learn more without giving away too much of what little he knows.

"He runs this city, or what's left of it. Spends his time rounding up Strags. He says the best and brightest have already left and everyone else should do the same. Rather insulting, don't ya think?"

"What about you? What do ya call yourself?"

"Names aren't a good thing to have in this place. They have a way of winding up in the wrong hands. Gives anyone looking for ya a piece of ID. They can use that to find ya."

"Why are ya here?"

"Keep an eye on this place. Watch for people like you trying to get in. Getting in without being caught is hard. And once ya get in, if ya get in, it's a maze of corridors and blind alleys. Easy to get lost."

"Mind if I call ya Signals? Ya okay with that?"

"Sure, whatever."

"Okay Signals, have ya been in there?"

"No, never."

"Then how do ya know what it's like inside?"

"Talk to the OTs. They used to work there."

"OTs, what's that?" asks Joe mimicking Signals' pronunciation, 'oughts'.

"Old Timers: retired BQT employees. If you're not a former BQTer, they call ya an OTnot."

"What's that mean, not an OT?"

"Not sure. Could mean ya ought not to go inside the place, or maybe ought not everything."

"Ought not everything?"

"Yeah, ya know. Ought not to," Signals searches for the right word, "exist," he concludes. "Maybe that's it. Ya shouldn't exist in their frame of reference. They're a strange bunch."

124

There's silence while Joe ponders this information.

"Anyway, if ya want to go in, ya need a map."

"Where can I get one?"

Signals pops out of the building entrance and scuttles away.

Dumbfounded at the sudden departure, Joe runs after him, following Signals into the shadow of a narrow alley wedged between two buildings.

"Ya want to stay under the radar," Signals explains. He looks cautiously around to make sure they are alone. "Can't be too careful." He reaches into his pocket and pulls out a wadded-up piece of white linen cloth with markings on it. "Here," he says, handing it to Joe. "It shows ya the main corridors and the layout of a few buildings. Ya can memorize what ya need. Ya can't keep it."

"Where did ya get this?"

"Drew it after talking to my SMEs."

"SMEs?"

"The OTs," says Signals, sounding annoyed because Joe doesn't understand what is obvious to him. "SMEs are Subject Matter Experts," he continues, warming to the subject. "They're familiar with the layout of the plant. They come by here and go inside. No one bothers them, if they stay out of the front office. Cornelius must have put out the word not to touch them. OTs got this nostalgia for a different time. Their memories of the place are sketchy. Each of them has a specialty, depending on which building they worked in. One will know the layout of a building and another is familiar with some of the connecting corridors. None of them has a comprehensive layout of the facility. Maybe Cornelius does. It gets tricky because the layout changed over the years. Depending on when an OT left BQT, they might not have a clear picture. More likely an OT has a snapshot of a particular time." His voice has taken on a professorial tone of one delivering a lecture to a student. "There are years of work left to create a comprehensive map."

Joe looks dubiously at the diagram, hoping to glean what he can from the second-hand information. He lets the would-be archaeologist continue. Signals is proud to share what he knows.

"The OTs talk in this weird lingo when they talk about the place and what went on inside. Sounded like gibberish at first. Ya can't trust them. They got this strange attachment to the facility."

In the feeble light of the alley, Joe squints at the map. He repositions it, hoping to put a better light on it. Joe is disappointed. "This isn't much to go on, is it?"

Signals flashes a look of annoyance. He knows there is only a handful of OTs that are willing to provide information and that creating a drawing from scratch would take months of effort.

"If ya can find a better one…" He lets the sentence tail off, not yet wanting to end their conversation. Unlike Joe, the Strags aren't interested in Signals' work. They want nothing to do with the place.

"What's this here?" asks Joe, stabbing at the scrap of linen. "It's labeled Aud."

"That's the auditorium. The OTs say they used to have departmental meetings in there when BQT was going full blast. They met with senior BQT people who explained what's what."

"How do ya know ya can trust what the OTs tell ya?"

"When it comes to the campus, they're reliable. They have this thing about being factual. It'll drive ya nuts."

"Why."

"They're very detail oriented. They talk about stuff at a minute level. They'll talk about a door when what ya want to know is what's behind the door. Is it a room, a hallway? What's in it? How big is it? Where does it go? Need to filter what they say. It's like they're looking at everything from the ten-foot level when ya want to see things from the hundred-foot level, like you're looking down from above."

"What's this?"

126

"Don't know. Couldn't get a straight answer from the OTs."

"What about this? The corridor ends abruptly in a blank space."

"Yeah well, the map's a WiP. Why ya going in there anyway? The OTs say there's nothing in there anymore except old, busted machinery."

"WiP?" asks Joe, becoming irritated by Signals use of obscure terms.

"Work in Progress," replies Signals, happy to show off his smattering of BQT Speak Think. "Hey look!" he whispers excitedly, as though having discovered a missing link in human evolution. "See there's one now. He's coming out."

A bent-over man in his late seventies emerges from the employees' entrance and totters off down the street.

"Who's he?"

"Don't know his real name. Call him Fuzzy, not right in the head anymore. Except for holidays and vacation, goes in five days a week almost the same time every day. Comes out later, like he's finished his shift. Haven't seen him in a couple of weeks. Must have been on vacation."

"What does he do in there?"

Signals shrugs. "Don't know exactly. Mostly they wander around, trying to remember the good old days when BQT was a booming enterprise."

"Have ya talked to Fuzzy?"

"Yeah, he's like all the rest. Talks in that strange language they have. Be careful, if you're talking to OTs. They're not always friendly. Helps if ya speak their lingo."

"You speak the lingo."

"A little. If you're planning on partnering with one of those guys to guide ya, forget it. They resent OTnots reminding them what happened to BQT. They want to remember the glory years. Some'll turn ya in, lead ya to Cornelius. Watch out for the OTs. They can be dangerous. There was one OTnot used to hang out around here. Most

127

called him Shakey. He wanted to go into the place with one of the OTs acting as a guide. Said he knew who this Cornelius guy really is. Said he wanted to prove it. He tried what you're thinking. He went in with an OT. Not sure which one. Could've been Fuzzy, maybe Slang, Wild-card Ricky, or one of the others. Who knows? Didn't see him after that. Maybe he's still in there."

"I was thinking you and I could go in together. Ya could translate, if we run in to one of the OTs. Opportunity for ya to explore first hand. You've never actually been inside."

"It's too dangerous. Why do ya want to go in there anyway?"

"I'm looking for Cornelius."

"Are ya one of the people he changed, gave a new ID? Hell, there must be millions of those, maybe billions. Best thing to do is let it go. Stay clear of the place. Make the best of the ID ya got. Create your own ID for that matter," says Signals in an accidental flash of brilliance. "If ya don't like him telling ya who ya are, then change it. Not going in there. You're on your own." Signals looks about nervously. He's itching to move on.

Joe continues studying the map. "Where would I find him?"

"Rumor is, he spends a lot of time in the Aud."

Joe steps partially out of the alley and looks down the long row of BQT buildings.

Signals yanks him back. "What are ya doing? Ya want him to see ya? Time to go. It isn't safe. Hand it over," says Signals, demanding the map. "Things happen in there. Once there was this silhouette in front of one of the windows." Signals jerks his head toward an endless row of broken windows. "Saw it for only a few seconds. Don't know what it was, but it was big. Ya wouldn't want to meet it in there."

"Wait. Look down there." Joe points to one of the distant buildings in the complex.

128

Signals eases down Joe's exposed arm. "Ya don't get it, do ya? If he sees ya, it's game over."

"No, down there," Joe persists. "There's a blind spot. Looks like an alley." Joe studies the map. "Yeah, here it is. What's down there?"

"It's a blind alley, no doors, no windows."

"What's this here?" Joe points at a small rectangle marked in the alley. The rectangle is labeled RE. "Is there a legend for this map? What's RE?"

Squinting, Signals looks over Joe's shoulder at the map. "Oh yeah, that's a Receiving Elevator. It's a freight elevator. It comes up through the ground. Pushes open a couple of metal doors over the elevator shaft. They used it to deliver supplies when BQT was in its prime. Leads to the basement. No map is going to help ya down there. The OTs say it's DGT. Don't know what that means. It can't be good. Don't recommend going down there. That's terra incognita."

"How do ya know?"

"Saw an OT disappear down the alley once. Never seen that before. All the others use the Employees' Entrance. Came back the same way a few hours later. Managed to catch up with him."

"And?"

"OTs have this single mindedness. They focus on the task at hand, especially when they're near the plant. They're almost completely oblivious to whatever else is going on. This guy was different."

"How so?"

"First off, he said his name was Link. That's unusual because OTs won't tell ya their names. Second, he smiled a lot. OTs don't smile. Asked him why he was smiling. He said SA. That means Situational Awareness. He described it as a larger awareness of your surroundings and circumstance. Then there was the third thing. He'd let loose this big laugh when he felt like it. OTs don't laugh. It draws attention. Ya don't want that around here. Makes ya nervous."

"What was so funny?"

"He said SM—that's Senior Management—tried to sell concepts to the employees when SM held what they called town-hall meetings. The Aud wasn't big enough, so management would bus everyone to the Inspire Megadome. Getting the workers in the same place was important because it made them feel proud to belong to something big and successful."

"Concepts?"

"Yeah, SM would push ideas like creativity in the workplace. The employees had no time to be creative. They were too busy churning out product to meet quotas and deadlines. Link said it was like telling someone to paint a picture or compose a song, then not giving them the time to do it. Even though SM spoke about creative building blocks like Situational Awareness, and IF—that's Imaginative Focus—they didn't really mean it. They didn't know what they were doing when they were preaching."

"Did Link say how to get in?"

"Yeah, ring the bell."

"Ever try it?"

"It's dangerous when ya start ringing a bell. Last thing ya want to do. Don't go there." Signals looks anxiously about. "Time to move. They'll be sweeping this alley soon."

"If I can get in through the elevator, there must be a way up to the first floor."

"Ya got a death wish? Got to go. It isn't safe. Hand it over," demands Signals.

Despite the map's unreliability, Joe reluctantly gives it to him.

Signals starts running up the alley.

"Wait!" shouts Joe.

Signals is about to turn a corner when he stops and starts dancing on the spot, like his feet are on fire. He's wants to get moving.

"What? And keep it down. Ya want them to know you're here?"

"There used to be a pawnshop in this neighborhood," says Joe, teasing out the tattered remains of a burnt memory. "Know anything about it?"

"Not a tour guide. Gone like everything else."

"What about the stuff inside the shop?"

"If you're looking for a gun for protection, FTS."

"What?"

"Forget That Shit. It won't help ya. Ya better learn the talk, if you're going in there. Otherwise you're DB."

"DB?"

"Dead Balls. Ya better start moving." Signals turns the corner and disappears.

Joe stoops and scurries to the nearest derelict car that takes him in the direction of the blind alley. He dives in through an open door, landing on the back seat. Not wanting to make any noise, he tugs gently on the door.

'Rrrrrrrreeeeeyt,' shriek the rusting hinges.

Joe jerks shut the door, abandoning all pretext of stealth.

'Bang,' says the door.

Joe peers over the back seat, looking for any signs of life in BQT headquarters. He checks the external cameras. They haven't moved. Huddled on the rear seat, he waits for the sun to drop below the horizon. Tired, he fights to stay awake.

Reap the Whirlwind

Joe wakes with a start. A car crawls by only steps from his hiding place. In a crazy game of hide and seek, an unseen hand jabs a searchlight at the streetscape. A shaft of light stabs at Joe's car. He checks his urge to run. The beam jumps to another target. He peers over the front seat at a pair of receding taillights moving in the direction of the blind alley. Looking over the back seat, he can see BQT headquarters with its office lights blazing.

He clambers out through a window. Following the prowl car at a respectful distance, he lopes down the street. Adjoining laneways and street paraphernalia offer sporadic cover. The vehicle stops a short distance beyond the alley. Joe ducks behind a derelict newsstand. The car lights snap off, leaving him in a black void.

Shuddering against the cold, he plots a path to the alley about twenty strides away. The street offers little concealment between his hiding place and the entrance to the alleyway. He weighs the possibilities.

The rumble of the engine cuts out. A car door swings open. A man exits, leaving the door open.

Joe crouches lower. He scouts his surroundings for a quick exit, if needed.

"Hey, where ya going? Ya know the boss isn't going to like it. Get back here," yells a voice from inside the vehicle. The voice sounds familiar to Joe, but he can't place it.

"Yeah yeah," answers the man on the road. "Taking a leak. Keep your shirt on. And keep your voice down."

"What's the matter, he got ya spooked?"

"He has a habit of turning up when you're not expecting."

"Now where ya going?"

"See if I can find a paper."

Joe hears footsteps getting closer.

"Hey! Get back in here!"

"Ya sound like my mother."

The voice is growing louder. Joe can't tell how close the man is.

"Why do ya read that rag?"

"These patrols are a waste. There aren't any Strags out here. And ya read the Lickspittle too. I see ya checking out the swimsuits. You're no fashionista either."

"I'm not the one going blind. Ya spend a lot of time reading the personals: 'Cougar looking for new play thing'."

"Ya seem to know a lot about it."

"Not as much as you."

"Hurry up will ya. We have to finish the patrol."

"Relax will ya? We got lots of time. Sun won't be up for another hour."

The door to a nearby newspaper box groans open and then slams shut. Joe can hear receding footsteps.

"Did ya get one?"

"Got two. Here's yours, so ya can check on your *friends*. Ya won't find any in Lore. This place is dead."

"Get in here. Close the door. Turn the heat on. I'm freezing."

"Yeah yeah."

The door slams shut. The engine jolts to life. A reading light snaps on.

Joe surveys the scene from his hiding place.

Now's the time, he decides. Taking a deep breath, he sprints toward the alley.

'TITITONGTONGTONGTONGTONG!' yelps an empty pop can, hurtling away from Joe's boot.

The searchlight stabs at the dark. The engine snarls. The tires howl. The car leaps forward looking for a place to turn around in the clutter of derelict vehicles. It lumbers through a U-turn. The engine roars.

Searching for the elevator, Joe paces back and forth at the rear of the alley.

"Come on! Where are ya?" he mutters.

'Ton, ton, ton.' 'Hey! Get your dirty boots off me!' protests the elevator doors.

He sweeps his hands over the wall.

The approaching car throws a feeble light into the alley, revealing a switch. Joe hits it. The riotous ring of a warning bell rips the night. A red warning light flashes.

Joe steps back.

The elevator doors remain closed.

The light intensifies. The dark is disappearing.

A crack opens between the doors.

The car squawks to a stop.

"There he is! Get him!"

Joe can hear approaching boots moving fast. He throws himself into the emptiness between the partially open doors, landing with a thud on the elevator floor. Scrambling to his feet, he slams a switch. The elevator stops and begins its sluggish descent. He pokes his head up, level with the pavement. Shielding his eyes against the light, he watches two shadows racing toward him.

'Ting, ting, ting.'

Joe ducks.

Staples smack the doors, ricochet and slam into the wall. Bricks burst and fly in all directions. Fragments rain down on Joe.

'Ting, ting, ting.'

More bricks rupture and fly apart.

Joe steps into the basement. The doors are almost shut. The light from above is almost gone. He spies a nearby electrical panel.

'Tung,' the doors conclude. The bell stops.

Joe pulls a lever, disabling the elevator.

'Bang, bang, bang!' Angry boots stomp and elevator doors thunder. The cacophony reverberates in the basement.

"Stand back!" shouts a voice.

'Teng, teng, teng,' yelps the barred entrance as staples rip through metal, and smash into the elevator floor. One of the staples hits a hydraulic line.

"That won't work! You're wasting ammo! Hey, pecker head! Your days are numbered!"

'Bang, bang, bang!'

"Yeah, you're messing with the wrong people! We're coming for ya! Prepare to reap the whirlwind!"

"Whirlwind? Who talks like that?"

"The old man and ya know he won't like him getting away."

"Where did ya get that idea? He said let him come."

"How do ya know?"

"Because he said so! Weren't ya listening?"

"Never mind! Let's go. I know a place."

Silence fills the basement.

Grumpy Pants

Joe presses against the damp basement wall. He has the impression that he's standing in a cavernous empty room, possibly a former warehouse.

'Click,' declares a circuit breaker on a distant electrical panel.

A row of fluorescent lights flickers on, illuminating Joe's presence. The rest of the room remains hidden. He scans for an exit. Seeing none, he ducks behind an enormous support pillar and peers down the corridor of light.

A man, appearing to hover just above the floor, glides quietly toward Joe. The stranger veers into the gloom, only steps from the pillar.

"YHNBbH! YerT!" croaks an accusing grumpy voice.

Joe does a quick about-turn.

A stooped, gnome-like figure, on an electric two-wheel scooter, rolls smoothly up beside Joe. Draped over his shrunken frame is a penny-brown uniform consisting of a work shirt and pants. Stenciled in glacier-white above a shirt pocket are the letters 'BQT'. With his work pants cinched high on his chest, the pant cuffs dangle above his ankles, revealing spindly legs. His socks droop, having lost their elasticity long ago. He wears a pair of decades-old work shoes. The dwarfish being dismounts his scooter and removes his bumblebee-yellow helmet. Wearing a permanent scowl, he brushes a rebellious wisp of parchment-white hair into place on an otherwise bald pate.

"What did ya say?" queries Joe.

"Ya have no business being here! You're trespassing!" the creature replies, switching to OTnotS (OTnot Speak) after accepting the futility of continuing the dialogue in Speak Think. "This is private property. Ya don't belong here."

"Are you one of the former employees?" Joe wonders if this in one of the OTs that Signals mentioned. Deciding that he is not, Joe christens him Grumpy Pants.

"What do you mean former?" Grumpy Pants challenges, bristling at the idea. "There's no such thing. And quit mumbling. Speak up. I can hardly hear ya."

"Are you an OT?" yells Joe.

"Ya can't stay here!"

"I was told that OTs don't come down here."

"Who told ya that, the mapper guy? What does he know?"

"I'm looking for someone."

"What?"

"I'm looking for someone," Joe hollers.

"Who, Mr. Millhouse?"

"Who's he?"

"The boss, Cornelius."

"Yeah, he's the one. How did ya know?"

"Never mind."

"Where can I find him?" Joe begins to feel the strain on his voice.

"Ya see that," snaps Grumpy Pants, observing a growing pool of hydraulic fluid beside the elevator. "It's busted thanks to your tomfoolery. Ya can't go back the way ya came. Follow me."

"Why don't ya point me in the right direction? I don't want to take up your time. Ya must be busy."

"Don't be stupid."

Grumpy Pants dons his helmet, mounts his scooter and silently sets off. The gnome circles back when he realizes that Joe isn't following him.

"Are ya coming?" he barks, glaring at the trespasser. "I don't have all day. I've got business to take care of."

"Wait a minute. What's this?" queries Joe, pointing to a hastily scrawled message painted on the support column.

"What's what?" asks Grumpy Pants, squinting at the declaration. "Oh, that. The little bugger was down here defacing private property. I fixed him." Grumpy Pants smiles with satisfaction before his face resets to its usual sullen demeanor. "Said it was a protest. It's none of your business anyway."

"To thine own self be," says Joe, following the message as it winds around the pillar. "He didn't finish it."

"You're damn right he didn't! I put a stop to his nonsense. He had no business writing on property that doesn't belong to him."

"True."

"Course it's true!" Grumpy Pants concurs. "Ya need to respect other people's property."

"No, I mean be true. To thine own self be true."

"What? I don't have time for this horseshit!"

"What happened to him?"

"The graffiti guy? He's in the Aud like the rest of the amateurs."

"Where's the Aud?"

"Let's go," demands Grumpy Pants, retaining a laser-like focus on his mission.

"What about your boss? Where can I find him?"

"Ya can't. Mr. Millhouse is busy. Ya won't find your way out by yourself," he declares contemptuously. "Ya can't be wandering around down here. It's a safety and security violation. Let's go."

Grumpy Pants glides away. Joe trots along beside him, having decided his best option is to follow along. The taciturn gnome leads Joe through a maze of dank dingy corridors. Grumpy Pants stops abruptly in the middle of a long hallway.

"Ya go through those doors," he directs, pointing at the other end of the passageway. "That takes ya into the old gymnasium. There's a basketball court. Go to the far end. There's a stairway that brings ya out onto the main floor. Turn right and follow the hallway until ya reach the employee entrance. Stay clear of the Aud. It's not your concern."

Joe feels uneasy about the unusually detailed directions coming from his otherwise taciturn guide. "Why don't ya come with me at least to the other side of the gym?"

Grumpy Pants hesitates. "Use your head! The scooter isn't allowed. It'll damage the floor."

"Maybe next time, ya can show me the Aud."

"What do I look like, your personal assistant? There won't be a next time," he scolds. "I'm cutting ya a break," he adds without conviction. Grumpy Pants turns around and heads off the way he came.

Tentatively, Joe pushes ajar one of the doors. He steps into the gym. The door swings shut.

Kffpp

Joe waits, letting his eyes adapt to the dark. He searches for a light switch. Not finding one, he follows the wall in pursuit of a stairway.

'Kffpp.'

An invisible force grabs his right pant leg and jerks it hard against the wall. He kicks to free his leg, but fails.

'Kffpp.'

A shirt sleeve is pinned to the wall.

'Kffpp. Kffpp. Kffpp. Kffpp...'

With each report, another body part is arrested. Even his head, pinned by his hair, is unable to move. Trapped, his only line of sight is parallel to the wall.

"Hello! Who's there?" hollers Joe, hearing the sound of receding footsteps. "Don't leave me like this!"

The footsteps stop. Joe's captor, flicks a switch, illuminating the circle at center court. The footsteps resume and then stop. Someone is standing under the light.

"Hi Borj. It's been a long time."

"Joe! The name is Joe! Ya got the wrong guy," he protests, struggling to free himself.

"Yeah yeah. Whatever. Do ya remember me? Probably not. The name's Stapler-Man, Stapes to those in the superhero biz. Any of this sound familiar? No? Doesn't matter. Call me Slash. I work for Cornelius now."

"Is he Identity-Man?"

"Never heard that one before. He's got lots of names."

"We could talk better, if I could see ya. Why don't ya remove..."

'Kffpp.'

An angry staple slams into the wall in front of Joe's face.

"Hey, be careful with those things! Ya could hurt someone!" Joe protests.

"Cutting edge stuff, these staples. Ya like my handiwork? Impressive, isn't it? I hate to be the bearer of bad news, but this is going to be a short conversation. I'm doing the boss a favor. He just doesn't know it yet. I can't figure out if he sees ya as a minor pain in the ass, or a real threat. Why's he got it in for ya?"

"I don't know that he has. Why don't I talk to him? Let me see if I can straighten this out."

"Too bad Razor isn't here. He's going to miss this. Well, he'll turn up eventually. To think that the three of us used to work out of the same office. Now look at us. Strange how things turn out, isn't it? When opportunity knocks ya have to grab it."

'Kffpp. Kffpp. Kffpp.' Three more staples slam into the wall. The last one grazes Joe's arm.

"Ow!" Joe cries, wincing from the sharp bite.

"Oops, did I nick ya?" asks Slash, feigning concern. "Didn't mean to. It's a minor flesh wound. That ought to do it anyway. Ya got any last words?" he adds mechanically, without any real concern for any wisdom that Joe might wish to impart before his demise.

"Look, let's talk this through!"

"I'll let my stapler do the talking."

'Kffpp.'

'Tink.'

"What the hell! Where'd you come from? Get the hell out of my way! Hey, get your hands off me!"

Joe can hear Slash slamming into exercise equipment in a far corner of the room, followed by moaning and then silence.

The pungent smell of a cigarillo hangs in the air. Someone is standing immediately in front of Joe.

141

"Who's there?"

Thank You

"Hold still, kid. This won't hurt." The newcomer speaks in short sharp bursts in the rhythm of a boxer throwing combinations of lightning punches.

"I've heard that before. Ya sure move quietly," observes Joe, wanting to make a connection. "Ya could be a one-man army with that kind of stealth. Ya saved my life. How can I repay ya?"

"Yeah yeah, relax. Ya already have. Ya talk too much."

"What did ya say?"

There's a humming sound. The staple in front of Joe's face is ripped from the wall, creating a small cloud of dust. The action is repeated for a few more staples, allowing Joe some limited movement, including his head. He sputters and coughs. After the dust clears, he turns his head to look at his rescuer. Astonished, he looks up.

"You're Disposal-Man," observes Joe, remembering a newspaper clipping tucked in Borj's journal.

The behemoth looks down at Joe, who can just make out the monster's face in the dim light. The face is an amalgam of charred, ovoid-shaped components, seemingly formed by tectonic forces. Some components appear compressed and rounded, and others stretched into elongated shapes. The face has a human quality, although disfigured by the small pressure ridges between components. Joe has the feeling that the architect was intent on constructing a self-portrait. He wonders who the creator was.

"You're staring," Disposal-Man calmly admonishes. "That's not polite."

"Hey! I'm breathing here!" Joe retorts. "Give me some room, will ya?"

Disposal-Man retires to the center circle where he arranges several chairs and seats himself. The metal chairs groan under his weight. He leans forward, rests his arms on his thighs and contemplates Joe.

"Last time we were this close, ya were looking at me though a cloud of flour."

"I can barely understand ya. Speak slowly," demands Joe, hoping to put the giant on the defensive.

"Yeah yeah, let me see what I can do. I don't get many visitors." The voice gradually slows as Disposal-Man talks. "Your speech has too many units. How's that?"

"Better. What are units?"

"You call them words."

"Maybe some time ya can give me a demo of your language."

"Sure, kid."

"Sounds like ya picked up some of the local lingo."

"People feel less threatened. It takes practice, fitting in. And for the record, it's Disposable, not Disposal. Intelligence at NPA mistranslated the symbol. Besides the two of us, there's only one other person knows about Disposable. Anyway, you and I got unfinished business."

Joe struggles to loosen the remaining staples. They refuse to budge.

"It's Cornelius I want to see. I don't have a beef with you. Why don't ya remove the rest of the staples?"

"If I remove them, ya might run. You're the one that put me in The Millhouse."

"I'm sure this Borj guy was only doing his job. If I am who ya think I am, and I'm not saying that I am, then no hard feelings, right? And how do ya know Borj and me are the same person?"

"Borj and I," corrects Disposal-Man. "I don't know that ya are Borj. Facial recognition isn't used where I come from. All of ya look the same to me. Slash thinks you're the one, so that's good enough."

"Slash isn't exactly an authority on who's who."

"Mind if I smoke?" asks Disposal-Man, opening one of his chest compartments. "Bad habit I picked up. It helps me fit in. Kind of like camouflage. I picked up a lot of bad habits from him."

"Who, Slash?"

"Mostly Cornelius. Smoke?"

"No thanks. It's bad for my health."

A groan emanates from the exercise equipment.

"Is he okay?"

"Yeah yeah, he'll be fine. He won't bother us," Disposal-Man answers, indifferent to Slash's condition. "I've been waiting for ya. Beginning to think that maybe ya wouldn't show." He lights his cigarillo and inhales.

"I wouldn't want to disappoint."

"Keeping busy in The Millhouse is important. I don't mean busy filling the hours while doing your time. I mean a direction." Studying his cigarillo, he exhales. "I need to quit. This is going to kill me."

"How did ya know I was coming?"

"At first I tried to figure out how I would make ya pay. Hate can eat ya up inside. It doesn't take much to get things rolling."

"Ya sound human. What happened to forgive and forget?"

"We're surprisingly alike. Anyway, back then I wanted ya to know what I was going to do to ya."

"We all have our goals and dreams."

"I had it all worked out. I wanted ya to have time to think about it. The imagination is a wonderful thing, isn't it?"

"Depends on who's doing the imagining." Joe is tiring in his fight against the staples.

"After that, I needed a new focus. I decided to learn about your world. I started reading the Lickspittle newspaper. I had lots to read in my papier-mâché prison. I couldn't move much. Paper has an inhibiting effect on my kind when present in sufficient quantities. I started by reading what was right in front of my face. Later, I repurposed a few small mirrors and a borescope; they're part of my in-field repair kit. I learned that with a few, minor contortions and the repurposed tools I could read a lot more. The papers were badly shredded. I had to read a fragment here and a fragment there to piece together articles. It took patience. Want to know what I read about?"

"Sure, looks like I'm not going anywhere. Ow!"

"Ya okay?"

"Leg cramp, I'm fine. Anyway, what did ya read?"

"There was one article. Took me months to piece it together. Ya know what it was about?"

"If it's the Lickspittle it could be anything. Let me guess, 'Dancing Walrus Released from The Millhouse'. Am I close?" Joe asks, having learned about Disposal-Man's release from an old edition of the Lickspittle during his journey to Lore.

"Don't know about a dancing walrus. That sounds farfetched. The article I read contained an interview with a guy who had sailed solo around the world. He returned to his home port after years at sea. A reporter asked him what he had learned. The sailor answered, 'The open ocean is a big place, but the heart is bigger. May you run true.' I don't know what he found out there alone on the water. It must have been enormous. I searched for other news articles about his sailing adventures. I found nothing."

"Can't help ya there. I'm kind of tied up," says Joe, calling attention to his plight.

"Then I started thinking about my own circumstance and experiences." Disposal-Man's voice has softened and faded almost to a whisper, creating the impression that he is somewhere distant.

146

Joe strains to hear.

"I realized that I needed to accept the events in my life for what they are. I needed to embrace life for all that it offers and not give up and turn away. Hold close to everything life provides. It's a gift. Use it wisely."

The room is silent.

"Thank you," adds the being.

"Why are ya thanking me?" asks Joe.

"I wouldn't have discovered the message without you." Disposal-Man gets up and walks over to Joe. "I wanted to return the favor by letting ya know what I learned. It's my gift to you."

Disposal-Man removes the remaining staples.

"Ya can go now, if ya like."

Disposable

With the removal of the last few staples, Joe slumps and then recovers himself.

"I think I better sit down."

"Good idea. You're a little wobbly on your pins," Disposal-Man observes. He helps Joe take a seat on one of the chairs before he too sits down. "Ya did me a favor. I owe ya for that."

"Where do ya come from?"

"It's a long story."

"I'm listening." Joe settles himself in his chair.

"My designation is GPDA, subclass MAAIU. Like all GDPAs, I'm affiliated with a TGC. I have fifteen MCIs to my credit."

"Whoa! Explain your terms. Otherwise it's gibberish to me."

"A GPDA is a General-Purpose Disposable Asset. They usually call us Disposables. MAAIU means Mission Assignable Actively Independent Unit. A TGC is a Trans Galactic Conglomernation, Tran for short. Each Tran spans countless galaxies. A Tran is part corporation and part government. It's hard to tell where one ends and the other begins. And where I come from, few try. Trans are entities unto themselves; a Tran is a Tran is a Tran. An MCI is a Major Conflict Interjection. You call it a war. When there was a conflict between Trans, I was sent in by my Tran. Ya were right when ya said one-man army. That's what I am. Only, where I come from Disposables are legion. There are billions of us. They crank us out on assembly lines in manufacturing facilities that cover entire planets. And when there's a conflict between Trans, each Tran sends in hundreds of millions of Disposables. They send us in and we get ground up like cars in a junkyard. Very few of us survive more than a couple of interjections. I'm unusual because I survived fifteen. That makes me a hero, or at least I was."

"When ya say affiliated with, what do ya mean?"

"One of the Trans created me. It owned me. They ID'd me down to the last quark of my DNA. That's Dynamic Nomenclature Authentication. The Tran can upgrade a unit's DNA at any time to satisfy the needs of the Tran. That makes it dynamic. Nomenclature is the terms or rules that define me. For example, Mission Assignable Actively Independent Unit are rules that define what I am and how I achieve my missions. I am a means to an end. What end I don't know. The official reason given by a Tran for an interjection is usually a motherhood statement about freedom, which is rarely the true reason. Authentication means that the Tran validates who I am. Without the validation, I would be nothing. I would have no purpose. Do ya understand?"

"Okay," responds Joe, looking a little perplexed.

"There was something in my last DNA upgrade," he continues. "Maybe it was a combination of the DNA plus all the components they replaced after so many interjections. I don't think they really knew what to expect. My architecture was ancient by then. Maybe there were incompatibilities."

"How old is ancient?"

"When I arrived on earth, I was one-hundred-thirty-nine earth-years old. Most Disposables don't make it to thirty. I spent most of my time fighting in interjections. The rest of my time was spent in CRDs, Component Replacement Depots. They keep CRD time to a minimum. If you're not engaged in an interjection, the return on investment is lower over the life of an asset. Think of it as part of the life-cycle management of a Disposable. The Tran wants to get the biggest bang for its buck. It helps keep down the average unit cost."

He reaches for a cigarillo. He stops.

"We start out like your child-soldier units." He contorts his face into a kind of smile, recognizing the absurdity of what he has said. Smiling doesn't come naturally to Disposal-Man. "We're purpose-built units, unlike yours that must learn how to be soldiers. We have it already programmed into us. Still, we both get trapped in interjections, or wars as you call them. GBD."

"GBD?"

"Get Busy Dying. That's the official motto of Disposables. We're a brotherhood."

"Are there others like you? I mean others that survived many wars."

"There were rumors that a few survived. The story goes the Trans didn't like them. It helps if ya understand our design. The Trans had to give Disposables enough autonomy to work independently on the battlefield without intervention by Central Command. Assets had to be able to innovate in order to complete their objectives. Independently of one another, each Tran designed a program generally known as FS, Fearful Symmetry. FS allowed a Disposable to see almost infinite avenues of opportunities for completing an assigned mission. Rookie units relied on a less sophisticated and less reliable set of algorithmic rules. If ya survived a couple of interjections, ya started looking for alternative ways to stay alive. That's where Fearful Symmetry comes in. Disposables that used it became unofficially known as FerS. They were nasty. Ya didn't want to face one on the battlefield. Some of the FerS started asking questions. It wasn't so much asking questions, it was the answers the FerS devised that the Trans didn't like. Eventually the questions led to the conclusion NR, No Rules. They learned to play each battlefield situation by ear. They developed an intuitive

150

sense of their SA, Situational Awareness. Unofficially, this approach to SA became known as Make It Up as You Go, MIUaUG."

"Fearful Symmetry sounds like imagination, creativity, spontaneity, with a narrow focus in your case."

"Yeah, that's a good description. The Disposables that used Fearful Symmetry started using MIUaUG off the battlefield. They were looking for answers. What am I doing here and why? That scared the shit out of the Trans because the answers didn't conform to Tran doctrine. A Tran wanted ya to believe that ya were free and the only way ya could stay free was by conforming to the Tran's dogma, whatever the dogma happened to be at that moment."

"What happened?"

"FerS started passing on what they had learned to other Disposables. There were stories of rebellions that Trans had to put down. The rebellions were small, a few galaxies in a Tran's theater of operation. Course a Tran faced with a rebellion kept it quiet. They didn't want other Disposables finding out. Trans were afraid the revolts would spread, if more Disposables knew about them. More importantly, ya didn't want the other Trans to know that ya had a problem. That's a sign of weakness, which made ya vulnerable to incursions by rival Trans. It was all hush hush. No one is quite sure what really happened. The FerS that took part disappeared."

"What about you? Were ya in on any of these revolts?"

"I liked to fly under the radar. And besides, I wasn't asking the questions the other FerS were asking. I did what I was told and kept my nose to the grindstone. It was easier and more comfortable doing what others expected of me. I stayed in my comfort zone. It kept everything simple."

"Why did the Trans bother with Fearful Symmetry, if it was so dangerous?"

"Each of the Trans would've done a cost-benefit analysis. They would've learned that Disposables that used

FS were far more cost effective than Disposables that didn't. The Trans started tinkering with RC."

"What's RC?"

"RC is Resource Choke. It's is a fusion of AI, Apathy and Ignorance, that dampens the full effect of Fearful Symmetry. Trans didn't like to acknowledge RC. Some of the Trans even put FS in their BRD, Basic Rights Document: All units shall have the right to bear FS. It was a brilliant move on the part of the Trans because the Disposables believed the right empowered them, made them free both on and off the battlefield. There was never any mention of RC. Even with RC, there were still revolts, so Trans kept tinkering with Resource Choke. They kept looking for a more effective version that would only inhibit Fearful Symmetry off the battlefield, not on. They must have given me an experimental version of RC. I guess the Tran figured that I was headed for DeCom soon, so here was one last opportunity to squeeze value out of an asset. DeCom means decommissioning."

"Ya still haven't told me how ya got here."

"I was in a cargo vessel, a freighter about the size of your moon. I had completed my last interjection. The Tran assigned me one last mission, DeCom. I was no longer cost effective. Technology had advanced significantly since I first rolled off the assembly line. Continuing to upgrade me was too expensive and time consuming; time is money. One way or another, DeCom happens to all Disposables regardless of the number of interjections. I was to be reconned."

"Reconned?"

"Melted down for scrap and reconstituted into whatever the Tran needed most. It happens all the time in TC, Tran Commerce.

"And?"

"I was down in the bowels of the freighter. Freighters are notoriously slow. If you're being decommissioned, there's no real hurry. I was in Austerity Mode to conserve energy. It's mandated by the Tran in fragile economic times when the Tran feels threatened, which is most of the time. Disposables must make sacrifices for the greater good of the Tran. I was surrounded by millions of Disposables, all of them falling apart and all of them about to be reconstituted, like myself. We were on our way to a DeCom planet. There happened to be a PJC on board the freighter. PJC is a Pro-tran Jingo Crew. Usually they record interjection events that are used for propaganda purposes. They showed up one day thinking that I might make a good backdrop for another story they were working on about everyone making sacrifices for the Tran. The PJCers didn't know that when you're in Austerity Mode you're still cognizant of your surroundings. They set up and took their shots. Essentially, I was wallpaper. There was a JT, a Jingo Talker, in the crew. The JT was reading the usual script with the usual values-based talking points: honor, duty, and resilience for the cause, whatever the cause was at that moment. The acronym that the Tran promoted was SFoD, Stay Free or Die. The JT kept using SFoD over and over in the presentation. Pretty soon the acronym began to sound like a nonsense word."

"Given your experiences, Stay Free or Die sounds ironic don't ya think?"

"Ironic?"

"Yeah, ya know. You're not free to start with and ya don't have much choice about dying."

"Yeah, that's it. SFoD is crap. Usually the cause was about staying free by defending the Tran against another Tran that was characterized as evil to the core. It was that sort of thing. Mostly it was about covering up the Tran's real purpose, EA, Economic Advancement. We Disposables had heard the storyline thousands of times concerning SFoD. Even Disposables can in time become skeptical."

"Then what?"

"The Pro-tran Jingo Crew left. They had what they wanted."

"And you?"

"I had a little time before the freighter reached the DeCom planet. I started using my base set of Fearful Symmetry to look at possibilities. The base FS doesn't consume enough resources that Austerity Mode will shut it down. I started looking at Resource Choke. I discovered that the routine could be overwhelmed in the interest of self-preservation. I managed to override the dampening effect of RC on the basis that the Tran was going to reconstitute me, which was a threat to my existence. When I did that, my full FS kicked in."

"What did ya do?"

"An idea came to me: Run! And I did. I escaped the freighter. The Tran hunted me. In their eyes, I was a rebel and dangerous. They managed to corner me in an old Transit Jump complex. A Transit Jump is an engine, a machine, used to transfer whole army battalions quickly from one galaxy to another when an interjection is required. The technology is not always reliable. Battalions that used it didn't always end up where they were supposed to. Some units were never found. That's not cost effective. The apparatus was later abandoned in favor of a faster and more reliable means of transport. I had time to initiate the engine's firing sequence. There was no time for calibration and to set a destination. I had only seconds before the Tran would have destroyed me. I jumped. When I came to, I was trapped in earth's gravity and falling. The heat was tremendous. I made a hard landing outside of Lore. My energy reserves were badly depleted. I needed fuel urgently. Cars were the best source I could find. That is until you came along with the titanium staples. They're an excellent energy source for a Disposable. That's why I went after ya, not that ya were a threat. I was after the staples. My low energy reserves slowed me down. I was limited to a slow speed over any distance greater than a couple of steps to avoid expending too much energy. That's why ya outran me on a tractor. I used almost all my remaining energy reserves in the silo. I figured I had ya trapped. That turned out not to be so."

"What are ya going to do now? Hang out here?"

"I've been studying your civilization. I've got a plan. I want to stop running away. I want to pick my battles, not let others tell me who I am and what battles to fight."

"Oh, what's your plan?" asks Joe, trying to hide his apprehension because he senses what Disposal-Man could do, if he chose.

"Your world has wealth beyond my civilization's wildest dreams."

Joe's alarm grows. He wonders if he has misread Disposal-Man's intent. "You're not thinking of inviting a Tran to invade to get in its good books, are ya?" he asks, with a look of disbelief.

"No, nothing like that. Where did ya get that idea? Besides, to a Tran, invading would not be cost effective. A Tran could collect all the resources in this galaxy in less than a century. It's not worth it. Your galaxy is too small and too far out of the way to make harvesting economically viable, at least not in the current conditions of Tran Commerce. And your galaxy is not militarily strategic."

"That's a relief," says Joe. He begins to relax a little.

"I mean literature, music, film, theater and the other arts. Ya have these treasures in abundance. Where I come from they don't exist. They're lost, if they ever existed. I want to take these things back and seed the galaxies. Think what these treasures could do. Think of the potential when combined with Fearful Symmetry. The possibilities are limitless. We could make our culture flourish in new and unimagined ways. Life doesn't have to be…," Disposal-Man stops to reflect, "dead. Yeah that's it, dead. Life is meant to thrive. It's a force greater than all others."

"How do ya plan to take them back with ya?" Joe asks, fearing that Disposal-Man will simply vacuum up all the treasures and physically take them with him.

"I have an almost limitless memory. I can store copies of your art in memory for the homeward voyage."

"How will ya get home?"

"I'm building a Transit Jump."

"Sounds dangerous based on what ya told me."

"Building one isn't too hard. The technology is simple where I come from. It's the calibration that's difficult because everything's in motion, the planets, stars, galaxies, all of it. Calibrating the engine can be done, if done carefully. I haven't the skill set or the resources to build anything more advanced than that. Why don't ya join me, help me build it?"

Joe is surprised and intrigued by the offer. Then he remembers why he's here. "I need to talk to Cornelius first. I want to know who I am. I'm hoping he can shed some light."

"I understand," says Disposal-Man. "He's in the Aud. He's waiting for ya. I think he's looking forward to seeing ya. I don't know why."

"Where can I get in touch with ya, once I'm finished here? I'd like to help ya with your Transit Jump."

"Here." Next thing Joe knows, Disposal-Man has impressed an address and map into Joe's memory.

"Thanks. I think," says Joe, feeling a little woozy.

"Don't worry. You'll be fine in a minute."

Slash stumbles to an exit and slams the door behind him.

Joe looks concerned. "Should we go after him?"

"I wouldn't worry about him. Cornelius told everyone to lay off ya and let ya come. Slash and Razor were acting on their own initiative. I dealt with Razor earlier. They're not a threat."

Having recovered, Joe stands up. He is about to leave when a thought occurs to him. "Do ya have a name other than Disposal-Man?"

The being is startled by the question. "I hadn't thought about it." There's a moment of silence while the unit thinks. "Neil, call me Neil. That's the sailor's name."

"Okay, Neil."

"Be careful. The Aud is up the stairs and to your left."

Pizzauff

A narrow stairway discharges Joe into a long, empty corridor on the first floor. Morning light spills in from a skylight running the length of the ceiling. He is only steps from the main doors to the Aud. Cautiously, he pulls on one of the doors and peers in. Before him is a vast room that could easily swallow a jumbo jet. The houselights are muted. Rows of seats extend to the foot of a giant, darkened stage. Thousands of spectators, each wearing a set of headphones, are seated randomly throughout the great hall; their lifeless faces immersed in the flickering cold light from tiny TV sets bolted to the seats. All are engrossed in the same program, *Guardians of the Free*. An episode is ending.

Joe quietly steps into the Aud. The door swings shut behind him. He waits for his eyes to adapt before slipping into a seat that he finds very comfortable. None of the ethereal beings turns to look at him. Curious, he puts on a set of headphones, and presses a well-worn, oversized, glowing red button labeled ON. Immediately the TV screen pops on, bathing Joe's face in the same strange luminescence.

The next installment of *Guardians of the Free* begins. The episode is entitled 'The Scummy Rats Within'. It opens, like all episodes, with a stirring rendition of the song *After Me You're First*. Extolling the rightness of common-sense values and oozing confidence, even the frailest and, by extension, the most hard-hearted watchers weep passionately at the syrupy music dripping from the

158

headphones. There is talk of making the song the national anthem.

The program is set in the not-too-distant future where the protagonists, Rip, Lance and Becky, work for a private agency called If It Ain't Broke Don't Fix It, IIABDFI. The government has commissioned IIABDFI to hunt down subversives, who seek to undermine the basic principles on which the fictitious country, Pizzauff, is founded. The basic beliefs are defined in Pizzauff's UPT, United People's Testament. A grim-faced announcer warns against the dire consequences should any one person or group attempt to circumvent or alter the fundamental tenets of the UPT:

All men, and women too for that matter, are islands and have the right to remain so.
No man can take what is not his, unless the guy who owns it says it's okay. Same goes for women.
Men are not equal except in the biblical sense when standing before God, unless you're an atheist or agnostic and then you're on your own and may God have mercy on your pathetic soul. Ditto for women.

The bit about being an island is the sacrosanct premise for minimal intervention by the state in the lives of all Pizzauffians. The piece about not taking another guy's stuff without permission is the basis for all commercial trade in Pizzauff. These two principles combine to define an economy in which the state is told to butt out of everything except matters related to national security. The final principle recognizes that God is supreme above all else and all Pizzauffians have an equal chance to make it big in the eyes of God, if nowhere else. In the series, God is presented as the consolation prize for weaklings, who fail to prosper from the boundless bounty offered by Pizzauff. These timid souls have no one to blame but themselves for their tribulations. And, truth be known, God favors the strong.

Fortunately, consolation prizes of any kind are reviled by sensible Pizzauffians, who believe that winning is everything. Pizzauffians are highly competitive, the result of the first two UPT principles. Hence, there are lots of weaklings because not everyone can have it all. Weaklings are despised because they are weak, for lack of a more contemptible word. Naturally, Rip, Lance and Becky, with their win-at-any-cost spirit, personify all things cherished by the staunchest believers in the UPT. Consequently, the trio often work at cross purposes when chasing down bad guys because they are highly competitive. For the most part, cooperation is not an option, except in the most horrific circumstances when the country is about to be ripped apart by one of its many enemies.

Their competitiveness helps explain the motto of Pizzauff, 'Dog Eat Dog' or DED for short. DED appears prominently throughout each show, most notably on the uniforms worn by the IIABDFI agents. DED was introduced by a writer for the series under the auspices of the show's executives. At the time, no one associated with the production of *Guardians of the Free* recognized the aspersion accidentally leveled at the fictitious citizens of Pizzauff and, by extension, the rabid fans of the show. Production costs being what they are, the expense to eradicate DED from the low-budget show is prohibitive. Fortunately, over time the TV viewers have forgotten what DED means. Now, everyone is living happily ever after except for the writer, who, to the revulsion of the show's executives, turned out to be a subversive and a weakling. He was fired by a low-level employee from Human Resources. The show is doing very well financially. It's in its fifth season.

After watching for a few minutes, Joe twists the channel selector. He discovers that all the channels are playing the same episode. Forgetting why he is here, Joe relaxes and watches, curious to see what will transpire.

160

The show's formula is the same for each episode. Intelligence agents Rip, Lance and Becky spend their time hunting domestic terrorists who want to change the United Peoples' Testament. All three agents are highly trained, having advanced degrees in subjects that would make your head spin. The agents' dedication is a marvel to watch. Using super-advanced, high-tech gadgets, they methodically seek out those bastards who are bent on undermining the core beliefs cherished by all correct-thinking Pizzauffians.

In contrast, the enemies of the state are a ragtag bunch of evil doers that want to add seditious amendments to the UPT. Here are some examples of their proposed wrong-headed thinking:

> *Everyone has the right to bear imagination and use it whenever they like.*
> *Everyone has the right to think outside the box.*
> *Kick the shit out of the dark until the light shines through.*

These despicable idiots, with their crack-brained ideas to subjugate the masses, are mockingly branded intellectuals, who witlessly conspire against the state. Like rats, they scuttle about in basements and attics hatching their evil plans. At the eleventh hour, when the ravings of these lunatics are about to tear the country to shreds, Rip, Lance and Becky grudgingly coalesce into a cohesive team, develop a counter-terrorist plan with a code name like Shit-kicking Thunder, and kick the crap out of the wannabe revolutionaries. The radicals, in their delirious ravings, vociferously claim to be writers, artists, musicians, etc. No one's buying it, least of all the audience.

The protagonists gush with pride from every pore of their being after laying down some righteous justice on the demented elements within society. Vigilance is the watch word, if loyal citizens are to remain strong, proud and free, though mostly proud.

Finally, to square the circle, the show ends with a token nod to God. In the script for each episode, the scene is always entitled God Only Knows. Rip, Lance and Becky are tasked with justifying the ways of Pizzauffians to God, so that He knows in his heart of hearts that Pizzauffians are doing their best against the Godless horde. This God moment is a concession to the God-fearing viewers.

Amazingly, the most comatose onlookers are the strongest proponents of the outcome. They smile fanatically and fervently nod agreement despite their feeble condition, while they wait with pee-in-their-pants excitement for the next installment in the series to begin.

Joe is astounded and overwhelmed by his own feelings of triumph and vindication over the evil forces that threaten the rightness of Pizzauffians and everything they hold dear. Transfixed, he waits eagerly for the next episode.

"Did ya like it?" poses a voice next to Joe's ear.

Joe tears off his headphones and twists around in his seat. A face looms large before him. Joe recoils like a loaded spring.

The Falcon and the Crow

"Good to see ya, kid. Did I scare ya? I didn't mean to." Cornelius leans back in his seat. He wears a thin satisfied smile. "I saw ya sitting here, so I sat down and waited for your show to end. Now, here's the ten-dollar question: do ya know who ya are? No? Then I'll tell ya. You're who I make ya," he says with authority. "And right now, you're…" There's a pause while Identity-Man tries to remember. "Let me think. Don't help me. I'll get it," he insists, his eyes dancing like sparklers. "Norm. Yeah, Norm," declares the king of the grifters. "That was close. I had a brain fart. Almost forgot."

"Joe. The name is Joe."

"So how are ya? Kind of like old home week, isn't it? Ya want to watch some more TV? I can come back. There's no hurry."

Joe has a feeling that despite what Cornelius says, he's eager to get on with whatever he has planned.

"I think I've seen enough." Joe feels for an off button without taking his eyes off the consummate con man. Finding only the ON button, he presses it. The TV screen remains on. The next installment in the series commences.

"If you're looking for an off button, it doesn't exist. Most don't want to turn it off. It does have a sleep mode. Makes the screen go blank. Saves energy. It's great technology, real slick shit. Monitors eye movement. You're probably dead, if it goes into sleep mode. Though sometimes ya get a false positive. Ya should see the look of panic when that happens to one of them. They don't want to miss even a second of the show. Their loyalty is amazing, incomprehensible when I think about it. It's fun to watch when one of them gets a false positive. There was one the other day. Guy got this stunned look, like his miserable life was flashing before his eyes. Then he realized all he needed to do was hit the ON button. Ya should've seen him slap that button. Bang!" Cornelius yells, clapping his hands and surprising Joe. "I swear he had the reflexes of a cat," he observes, laughing. He starts coughing, then manages to stop.

"What do ya do when a series ends?"

"I got other series. I got one about zombies for instance. Do ya like zombies? Lots of people do. Here's a fact for ya." He leans forward confidentially. "Zombies are misunderstood. They're like everyone else, no different. The eyeballs eat them up; can't get enough of them." He leans back, wearing a satisfied smirk. His eyes beam like Christmas lights on steroids.

"Eyeballs?"

"The more *genteel*," he sneers, "call them viewers. I call them what they are. It's all about head count, the more the merrier. And speaking about comedy, I got a series about Adam and Eve, only their names are Jack and Jill, J and J for short. Show's called *The Stumble Bums*. Mysterious visitors keep dropping in on them and then things get mixed up. It's a zany comedy of errors," he declares, sounding like a commercial. "Every episode it's the same old thing. J and J keep falling for the same old gag with the same old pratfall. Ya would think they'd begin to see the pattern, but they don't. The eyeballs love it. They start behaving like the characters in the show. That's subliminal programming for ya. It's great propaganda." Chuckling, he shakes his head in disbelief. "The show's predictable and cheap to make. It's a great money maker. All ya have to do is keep your costs down to maximize profit and you'll do fine. Oh, I almost forgot. I have full-length feature films too. I got one about…"

164

Lost in thought as the flimflam artist proudly hawks his wares, Joe doesn't know what to believe. His world is crumbling before him.

Who is this old fart, Joe wonders? *What's he up to?* Joe stares off into space, as if the answer might be there. *Who am I? I thought the answer would be easy. A couple of minutes with him were all I needed to figure it out, but he doesn't know any more about who I am than I do.*

"Hey, Norm, pay attention!"

"I was thinking," Joe responds. He decides to play along.

"Well, listen when I'm talking. Ya asked a question and I'm giving ya the answer. I'm doing this for your own good," Cornelius adds, sounding peeved. Then, catching himself, he dons the mask of affable emcee.

"Okay, I'm listening."

"Anyway, I got all kinds of shows. Today it's *Guardians of the Free.* Tomorrow it'll be something else. I have my minions working all the time."

Cornelius stands up. "Why don't we go to my office where we can talk? Come on. I'll show ya. It isn't far." He walks to the aisle. Turning to look back, he gestures warmly, coaxing Joe to join him. "Ya coming? You'll like this. I got ya a present," the fraudster appends as an inducement. "And no more zapper, I promise ya, cross my heart. That's history."

Joe remains seated, unsure if he wants to follow. He has an uneasy feeling in the pit of his stomach about the zapper, but can't put a memory to it.

"Ya remember the zapper don't ya? No? Well, never mind. Let's go."

Joe joins him in the aisle. "What are ya going to do?"

Casually, the huckster pulls out a cigarillo and lights it. "Follow me. I'll show ya." The grand marshal heads quickly down the aisle toward the stage.

Pulled by the downward slope of the aisle, Joe trudges behind, following a cloud of smoke.

Halfway down the aisle and gasping for breath, Cornelius stops. Unexpectedly, he hunches over, placing his hands on his knees for support. Soon he's consumed by a full-on, rib-cracking, coughing fit. Cornelius looks like he's about to disintegrate into a heap of ash.

Joe looks on anxiously. Searching the nearby TV watchers for any sense of concern, he wonders if he can expect any aid, if needed. Their gaunt faces are riveted to the TV screens. They ignore the plight of the incapacitated Cornelius. Joe tries to steady him. Finally, the coughing subsides.

"Ya okay?" Joe lays a comforting hand on Cornelius' back.

From his stooped position, the crippled Cornelius nods yes, unable to speak. His chest heaves as he gasps for breath. His body shudders. "Yeah, I'm okay," he wheezes. A few minutes later, he pulls himself upright. "I'm better now."

"Ya need to cut down on the smoking before it kills ya."

"That's the least of my problems," he chuckles cautiously, not wanting to induce another coughing episode.

"Ya sure you're okay?"

"Yeah yeah, I'm fine! Stop asking," the curmudgeon snaps.

He resumes his determined march only to stop again. "In front of the staff, call me Mr. Millhouse. It's a sign of respect."

"Okay," Joe responds.

"Okay what?"

"Mr. Millhouse."

"That's better." Joe's host smiles. "You'll notice I believe in positive reinforcement. That's an important lesson."

Joe isn't sure if his decrepit leader is taking on the role of mentor, or indulging in self-promotion.

Confronted by a short flight of stairs at the front of the stage, Cornelius calls a halt to the two-man parade. "After you," he says.

Joe mounts the stairs.

"Now, give me a hand up. I have trouble climbing stairs. I was sick when I was younger. It affected my heart. Going down is no problem."

Joe extends a hand. Cornelius latches on with his patented grip of death. Joe pulls him gently up the stairs and onto the stage.

"There, that wasn't so bad," decides the master of ceremonies, turning to look at the throng below. "Nice crowd," he observes. "They're a dedicated bunch."

Joe looks out at the blank faces. "Looking a little tired."

"No, I'm fine."

"No, I mean the people sitting down there. Do ya ever give them a break? They look like they could use it."

"They're okay. Besides, they're free to come and go whenever they like. Occasionally one'll bite the dust. Pretty much wasted away to nothing by the time one of them gets hauled away. Don't weigh more than a stale loaf of bread. No substance to them in the end. Ya got to get rid of them before they stink up the place. I make Slash and Razor cart them out of here. The head count dropped this morning."

"Don't ya think ya should help them before they're too far gone?"

"Help who?"

"The eyeballs. Don't ya think ya should help them?"

"What! Help them?" the con artist retorts with disdain. "No, it's up to them. Never mind them. Let's get down to business. Hey Razor!" he yells, looking offstage. "Where are ya? Give me some light and bring that case out here. Come on, let's go. I haven't got all day."

The stage lights shatter the dark, momentarily blinding Joe.

Slash limps on stage carrying a battered, black case. Glaring, he walks straight to Joe at center stage and stops. Joe is a little unnerved by Slash's presence.

"Well, what are ya waiting for? Put it down!" Cornelius growls. "Then ya can go. And next time I tell ya to lay off someone, ya do it. Norm here is none of your concern. Ya got that?"

"Yes, Mr. Millhouse," mumbles Slash with a hangdog look. He sets down the case and hobbles off stage.

"Wasn't that Slash, not Razor?"

"Could be. I can't tell them apart. Never mind that. Open it up. See what I got ya. I went to a lot of trouble to find that. I hope ya like it."

Joe opens the case. Inside is an alto sax. He is unsure what he is expected to do with it.

"Ya like it? Ya don't remember do ya?" Cornelius asks, sounding disappointed. "That was your weapon of choice. See here. It's got a big B on it. That's B for Bazooka." He looks at Joe expecting at least the glimmer of a chuckle from him.

Joe is unresponsive.

"Okay, it's B for Borj. Thought ya might appreciate my joke, given your former line of work as a superhero. Work on your sense of humor, will ya?"

Impulsively, the hustler reaches into one of his pockets. Pulling out a crumpled newspaper article, Cornelius unfolds it and offers it to Joe. "Here, take it. This'll convince ya." The article includes a picture of Borj in his superhero costume. He's pretending to play his saxophone for the benefit of the photographer. "Found her in a pawnshop. They were having a closing out sale. Moving to Pawsoff. I got a good deal. It's yours now. Go on, try it," he encourages. "See what ya can do."

With a little prompting from Cornelius, Joe assembles the instrument. It has an oddly familiar feel.

Joe looks doubtfully at the sax. "I don't know how to play this."

168

"Sure ya do. It'll come back to ya. Some things ya can't erase; well, not totally. And believe me, I've tried. I'm betting it's still in your DNA. Trust me. Try her for me," he coaxes. "Show me what ya got. We can do a play-in to get ya started. Look, I got a sax too. Where's my sax? Slash! Give me my sax."

Razor limps on stage. He hands the sax to his boss.

"Now go find a seat. Ya know the one I mean. And what the hell happened to you? Never mind. Just do what I tell ya."

"Yes, Mr. Millhouse."

Razor hobbles down the stairs and heads to the back of the Aud.

The influence of *Guardians of the Free* and the infectious enthusiasm engendered by Joe's Machiavellian host make a heady brew. Joe wonders if he might have a chance to lay a righteous beating on the little weasel for his treatment of the eyeballs. Payback time, Joe coldly calculates.

"Okay, let me warm up first." Joe answers, trying, with limited success, to hide his contempt.

"That's the spirit! Go for it!" Cornelius encourages, ignoring Joe's scorn.

Tentatively, Joe blows a note. Astonished by the result, he plays a few more notes and then still more. The notes fill the Aud. As predicted, the music floods into Joe.

"See! Didn't I tell ya? I knew ya had her in ya!" exclaims the savvy swindler. "Oh, I still know a thing or two. Next time I tell ya something, listen up and do as you're told. Here, see if ya can follow this."

Cornelius begins playing. He's good. Joe eagerly joins in. Their notes intertwine and play off one another. Occasionally, Joe's fingering stumbles before recovering. The song becomes more intricate with each note. Just when Joe thinks he's in synch, Cornelius fires off a new and more complicated passage, leaving Joe scrambling to catch up. They stop after several minutes.

"Not bad" concludes the master musician.

"You're not so bad yourself, for an old geezer," says Joe, feeling smug.

"Geezer! That's hitting below the belt. Well, never mind. I've taken worse shots than that. Did I mention there's a set of eyeballs down there that ya know?" asks Cornelius, setting up a counterpunch. "Go on. Have a look."

"Where?" Joe asks, caught off guard.

"Over there. Hey, throw a spot on her," he barks at the offstage Slash.

A spotlight jumps to life. Its beam plays over the crowd, coming to rest on Razor. He is only a few seats distant from where Joe sat. Grinning, Razor casually drops his arm on the backrest of the seat next to him.

Joki pays no attention to Razor's arm. She's focused on the TV show.

"How's she doing?"

"Not good, Mr. Millhouse," hollers the grinning Razor. He sniffs. "She smells a little overripe. She won't last much longer by the look of her."

Feigning astonishment, Cornelius turns to Joe. "Ya were sitting almost right beside her, your own sister. I'm shocked ya didn't recognize her." He shakes his head in disbelief. "Hey," he shouts, "best estimate. How long has she got?"

Razor assesses Joki. "Don't know, Mr. Millhouse. Not long, maybe a day," yells Razor. "Maybe less. Hard to tell when they're this far gone."

"How much is in the pool?"

"Almost a hundred, Mr. Millhouse," shouts Razor.

"Put me down for another twenty."

The bringer of death beams at Joe. "Now I can see what you're thinking. Is that really her? It's been a while since ya last saw her. Do ya remember? Ya probably don't."

"You're right. I don't recognize her. How do ya know it's her?"

"I know a lot of things. More than ya can possibly know. See, it's like this. There are things ya know that ya know for certain. There are things ya think ya know, but don't. There are things ya know that ya don't know. And there are things that ya just don't know. Got it? Simple, right? And there isn't much that I don't know. The truth is, there are very few surprises left for me."

Joe's head is beginning to spin. "Ya missed one."

"I don't think so. What?"

"You said it yourself with your talk about DNA. Ya didn't say it in so many words. Remember?"

"Nope. Enough with the riddle. Let's hear it."

"There are things ya don't think ya know that ya do know."

"You're right. That's one for you," confirms the trickster, reaching into his pants pocket.

Joe tenses.

"Relax. I said no zapper this time. I'll keep my end. Don't ya trust me? Here," he says, tossing Joe a crumpled newspaper article entitled 'Borj's Muse Revealed'. It includes a picture of Borj and Joki. Beneath the picture, Joki states 'I help sometimes. I give him a nudge in the right direction when he needs it.' "She wandered in here one day and sat down. I couldn't believe it. It happened shortly after I sent ya to that little backwater place, Outhouse Bay."

"Away Home Bay," Joe corrects.

"Whatever. She's been here ever since."

Pausing for a moment, Cornelius feels inspired. "Here's a nature lesson for ya. Did ya ever watch a falcon when it's hunting a crow?"

"What's that got to do with anything?"

"The falcon sees the crow off in the distance and the crow sees the falcon," he begins eagerly, with spittle flying in all directions. "The crow doesn't recognize that the falcon is a threat because the falcon is using motion camouflage. It masks its approach to the crow, so the crow flies on not paying much attention to the falcon. The reality is that by the time the crow recognizes the threat, it's too late. The falcon has closed the distance. It's all over for the crow. That's nature for ya, 'red in tooth and claw'."

Joe stares blankly.

"Ya don't get out enough," the storyteller observes with a look of incredulity. He curls a disdainful smile. "WHAM!" he hollers with a clap of his hands.

Joe jumps, startled.

"Isn't it marvelous the adaptations that nature makes?" He wipes his mouth with his shirt sleeve.

"What's your point?"

"Nothing really. Ya could ask your muse. Unfortunately, she's preoccupied. That's too bad."

Cornelius picks up his sax and plays a few bars. "Ya like it? It's called *Twisting Path*. Created it myself. Tell ya what. I'm feeling generous because I like ya. How would ya like to walk out of here and take your sister with ya? No tricks."

"What's in it for you?"

"Ya could do me a small favor. Ya give me what I want, and you and your sister are out of here. A couple of eyeballs won't make any difference to me. I got lots. Ya interested?"

"What is it ya want?"

"Information. I want the address that the Disposable gave ya. That's not so hard. Think it over."

Keeping his eye on Joe, the counterfeiter wends his way through *Twisting Path*. Finally, he stops. "Well, times up. What'll it be?"

"Why do ya want it?" asks Joe, who is having difficultly thinking clearly.

"It's time for me to go home."

"Isn't this your home?"

172

"You're joking! Look Norm, or whatever the hell your name is, I was exiled here a long time ago on this ball of dirt in this nothing galaxy. I needed a hobby to kill time while I waited for a ride home. I knew one would turn up eventually. I had to be patient and that's hard for me. I needed to keep busy in the meantime. Idle hands are the devil's workshop ya know. I decided to get comfortable while I waited, so I built everything ya see here. Not bad considering the limited resources."

"Wait a minute. Are ya telling me ya built Lore? That's not possible," Joe challenges, remembering an article in the Lickspittle. "The city was founded by some guy whose name escapes me."

"Ya mean Cyrus, Cyrus Caesar Millhouse?"

"Yeah, that's the one."

"That punk! Yeah, course he built it. Who do ya think told him to build it and everything else ya see? I hired lots like him."

"He was working for you?"

"Course he worked for me. I even made him change his name to Millhouse for legal reasons. The truth is, he was a ME man through and through. I made sure he had a bang-up funeral when he kicked off. He earned it. Politicians, celebrities, and lots of famous people came from all over to pay their respects. He chose the Caesar part. He was full of himself."

"How old are you?"

"I'm old, older than ya can imagine. And don't get any ideas about taking over. I'm not in any hurry to retire. Don't think I could if I wanted to. The management wouldn't allow it. Besides, being a super villain has its privileges. And for the record, super villain is a misnomer. I'm a superhero. I give people jobs and put food on the table. The fact is, I had to make a lot of people do things they didn't want to do. Some took a little *convincing*, if ya know what I mean. Others were more willing, like the Cyrus kid. Which are ya? Ya want to take the easy way, or be a hard ass? Think of your sister too. She comes in handy, doesn't she? Ya couldn't have done what ya did to the Disposable without her."

"What do ya mean?"

"She was the one that told ya how to trap the Disposable. At least she gave ya the spark for the idea. I got the information straight from her. We've had some good talks the two of us. Sometimes I think she's more dangerous than you. Without her, ya didn't stand a chance against the unit. I'm willing to give her up because that's the kind of guy I am, Mr. Magnanimous." He laughs. His laughter resounds throughout the hall.

"What do ya care which way I choose?"

"I don't. I'm easy either way. What matters is, I've got a ride home. I was lucky there. I didn't realize how lucky I was when the Disposable first showed up. It fell out of the sky, manna from heaven. I hadn't counted on ya capturing it. I got greedy. Not that there's anything wrong with that. I figured I could earn a few extra bucks through the National Protection Agency. Ya see, the city pays a base fee, regardless of whether ya catch the super villain or not, and a bonus, if ya manage to dispose of the villain. I had the agency send out one of you super buffoons. I never expected to get the bonus. Ya got guts. I'll give ya that. Ya did the near impossible. I didn't think ya had it in ya."

"What happens to Neil?"

"Who the hell is Neil?"

"The Disposable, what happens to him?"

"Why didn't ya say so? I can handle that." Cornelius pulls out his remote control. "It's a handy little gadget, like one of those whatchamacallit utility knives. They gave the zapper to me in a moment of weakness when they exiled me. If ya ever get marooned, make sure ya got one of these. It'll save your life."

"What about Neil?" Joe persists, looking apprehensively at the zapper.

174

"The Disposable needs a little re-programming once everything is built and calibrated."

"Sounds like the zapper is your solution to everything. It's like a hammer."

"What?"

"If your only solution is a hammer, every problem looks like a nail."

"It's the only tool I need. The reality is the Disposable has forgotten what it is. That's all. It'll make a reasonable messenger boy till I get a newer one. And where I'm going, I'm sure there are lots of new and improved models."

"So ya know about the Transit Jump?"

"Course I do."

"Why haven't ya used your zapper on him to find the location?"

"Can't. Zapper doesn't work that way. It would likely erase important information needed to calibrate the machine. I can't afford to take that risk. That's the thing I need most, the calibrating."

"Why don't ya ask him for a ride home?"

"It's different than most Disposables because it split from the program. And it suspects who I am. It'll never help me get home. That's why you're the key to all this."

"Me?"

"Don't look so stunned. I needed a way to lure the unit over here when it got out of The Millhouse. At the time, I figured it would be useful to have for my projects around here. That's where you come in."

"How so?"

"You were the bait," scowls Cornelius, becoming impatient with Joe, who seems incapable of following the most rudimentary elements of what the master schemer perceives as a simple plan. "For your information, disposables are very competitive. They don't like to lose. I figured the asset would be looking for ya when the prison officials released it. I figured it would want to settle the score because ya sent it to prison. I put out the word that I knew how to get in touch with ya. It was like blowing a dog whistle. When they released the unit, it came running, looking for information on your whereabouts. That's when I learned about its plan to build a Transit Jump. After that, I needed to keep a close watch on the Disposable because I wanted the engine once it was finished. I knew that if it thought ya were coming here, it'd stick around when it wasn't building the engine. That gave me more opportunities to find the Transit Jump. You were the incentive for the asset to keep coming back. I told it that I had sent ya a message and that ya were coming here. What could be simpler?"

"What message?"

"You're not paying attention. I sent a message by courier."

"I didn't get a message from any courier."

"Sure ya did, the guy with the hoodie. He was the messenger. I left a trail of breadcrumbs that even he couldn't miss. They led directly to ya. I even made sure he found your journal and your ID badge. Took a little scrounging. It was worth it though. I knew ya would come. Ya couldn't leave well enough alone, could ya? Ya had to know who ya are. Ya took your sweet time getting here. In the end, even that worked for me because the unit had more time to work on the Transit Jump. By my calculations, it must be well along in development."

"Did Monk know what ya were up to?"

"Who?"

"The guy with the hoodie."

"Him? You're kidding! He's in another world. Talk about naive."

"Why the trip to Away Home Bay in the first place? Why not leave me in Lore?"

"Got to be a lot of Strags here. They can be dangerous. I didn't want ya stumbling into a situation ya couldn't handle. I had to keep ya alive. Without ya, there was no incentive for the Disposable to come here. I had to put ya some place for safe keeping until I needed ya for bait. I wanted to send ya to Pawsoff so ya could work for ME, Millhouse Enterprises. That way, my ME operatives in Pawsoff could keep an eye on ya and ya could add a few extra dollars to the coffers working for ME. Ya owed me. I'd been carrying ya on the NPA payroll without getting any return on my investment. Then ya pissed me off at our last meeting."

"Johnny Magorey."

"What? You're not making sense."

"It's a nonsense poem."

"Never mind that. Pay attention to what I'm telling ya. Like I said, it's about knowing and not knowing. Were ya not listening? Ya need to learn to put two and two together. Ya have to adapt when circumstances change, so naturally the plan changed. I don't think ya got the instinct for business. You're too inflexible. It's all about evolving, survival of the fittest."

"That's what this was all about? I'm the bait, nothing more?"

"Yep," confirms the dean of the dodgers. "Everything was in motion and ya didn't see it coming, did ya?"

"And what about these people in the Aud?"

"Most of them were dangerous till I sucked them in here. They had curiosity and imagination. They refused to focus on what I wanted them to see."

"And what was that?"

"Are ya blind? This! All of this," says the monarch of the manipulators, gesturing wildly with an all-encompassing sweep of his arms. "I built everything ya see on this measly planet from scratch with my own two hands. The eyeballs didn't understand. They believed that BQT was a threat. I had to find a way to stop them. I tried finding them jobs at BQT working for me. Some of them were stubborn."

"Why didn't ya use your zapper?"

"In every crowd, there are always a few who are immune to my zapper. They have a built-in resistance. I don't understand why. It's a mystery. Most of those that refused to be accommodating I conned into coming in here. What suckers!" He shakes his head in disbelief at the ease with which he duped his enemies. "The rest is history."

"What happened? How did ya end up here?"

"Ya wouldn't believe the wealth and privilege I had where I come from. I ran things the way I wanted. There wasn't anyone big enough to take me down," boasts Cornelius. "There was a revolt in the upper echelons of my Tran. They got greedy. They wanted it all for themselves. They ambushed me."

"Coup d'état?"

"They'll pay. That's enough about me. Back to business."

"What happens to this world after ya leave, assuming ya make it back to where ya came from?"

"I'll make it back alright. Ya can count on that. And I plan on keeping this world too. It's like having a greenhouse where I can experiment and watch things grow. I wouldn't want to see it fall into a state of disrepair after I leave. I got a lot of sweat equity in this place. And I got people in place to manage the garden for me."

"Aren't ya concerned there could be a rebellion here, if ya aren't around to look after things?"

"No, won't happen. Hell, I'm a god to my minions. And besides, they won't have time to think about deposing me. I've rigged it so the ones I've left in charge will be too busy squabbling between themselves. They'll be like rats fighting over a chicken bone. It's all supply and demand. Like I said before, 'red in tooth and claw'. It's an easy lesson, except for a few like yourself that don't want to latch on to the concept. Ya lack passion, the will to make something of yourself. For Christ sake, man up! Be a part of this world. You're too easily sidetracked. Ya know what your problem is? Ya suffer from DLS, Distracted Living

Syndrome. It's like a disease, wanting to know who ya are. Though in this case, I managed to use your distraction to bring ya back to Lore."

Who is really being distracted here? Joe wonders, evaluating Cornelius.

"And oh yes," continues the old goat, looking derisively at the people seated in the Aud, "I got plans for them too. They're a threat to my garden, an infestation. And what do ya do with any infestation? Ya eradicate it." He smiles a hard smile.

Joe looks darkly at his enemy. "Let's go. I've heard enough. One more thing, I want the zapper too."

"Fill your boots," dares the maven of deception. "While we're at it, let's make sure everyone can hear this. Slash," shouts Cornelius, "patch us through to the headphones and drop a couple of mikes down here. And I want this recorded. I'm going to enjoy this."

Microphones descend, stopping in front of the two combatants.

"All set, Mr. Millhouse," shouts Slash.

"Hey, Eyeballs!"

Heads reluctantly look up at the stage.

"Pay attention to what I'm telling ya. This here is… What's your name?"

"Joe."

"This is Joe. We're going to play some music for ya. Listen up."

Cornelius immediately begins playing.

Joe scrambles to join in.

I'm with You

Gradually, Cornelius' music takes a disturbing direction, sounding like ball bearings in an industrial blender. Joe follows with his own version, mimicking a lawnmower blade grinding against a slab of steel.

Seeing an opening, Joe takes the lead, spitting out passages like volleys of nails. Bending the music to his will, he builds toward a soul-destroying note that will obliterate his enemy. Growing stronger with each note, Cornelius replies in kind with a cacophony resembling a train wreck. The dual continues for an hour, escalating to exploding grenades, mortars and cannon fire. Each bombardment grows progressively louder and more violent. With smiling eyes, the artful enticer blasts away, enjoying the interplay of their duet. Finally, Joe detonates his coup de grâce with a single note. The master of the con stops. Joe follows suit.

"Is that the best ya got? Hey Razor! How's she doing?"

"She's fading Mr. Millhouse. A lot of the rest of them are in bad shape too."

"Not doing so good are ya? I'm disappointed. Ya need a break? Ya look like ya had the shit kicked out of ya."

"Wait a minute. What's going on?"

"See for yourself." The skillful showman gestures at the audience. "That last shot of yours killed off a handful. I may need extra help to cart off the dead ones. Ya do good work. I appreciate the effort. Not everyone can fire off a note like that, except for me."

Joe looks with disbelief. Many of the onlookers are noticeably weaker than when the two of them started playing.

"If it's that easy, why don't you finish them off?"

"Can't."

"Why not?"

"Can't take what isn't mine."

"What about the ones you've already killed, the ones that sat there wasting away until there was nothing left of them?"

"Ooh!" The king of the melodramatic clutches at his heart. "That really hurts me to hear ya say that. I haven't killed anyone. I had nothing to do with their deaths. Every one of them chose. They were free to leave any time they wanted. I already told ya that. I resent your accusation!" he adds irritably. "Why are you so full of anger and hate?"

"Ya said yourself ya sucked them in here."

"Okay, maybe I exaggerated a little. All I really did was provide an *opportunity* for them to come in, sit down and enjoy the show. After that it was up to them. They could've decided not to come in. They could've left at any time. No one stopped them. It's called free will," Cornelius appends, smiling broadly. "You're doing a good job, but ya can do better. I appreciate your hard work. Good help is hard to come by. Go ahead, finish them," he coaxes. "You'll be doing them a favor at this point."

"It's you I want."

"Okay. Take your best shot. Give me your knockout punch. Go on. I don't think ya can take me." The champion of the hustle starts playing again.

Resigned to the inevitability of collateral damage, Joe picks up the thread.

Cornelius leads Joe through one vicious passage after another.

Joe looks out at the crowd as he plays. Slash and Razor are busy stacking lifeless bodies in the aisles. There are more bodies than the two of them can manage. OTs appear from alcoves and begin helping. The scene is more than Joe can take. He stops.

"Now what's wrong?" demands the frustrated Cornelius. "Ya were almost there. Get on with it!" The trickster resumes playing.

Numbed by the carnage, Joe's sax rests lifeless in his hands. "I've been conned."

Cornelius stops. "What? Course ya have. You're weak like the rest of them: no guts, no glory."

"I've been going about this all wrong. Haven't I?" A feeling of calm descends over Joe. "I've been dancing to your tune; letting ya lead me on, first with the TV and then the music. It's not me that's weak. It's you. Ya bully people into believing they're not who they are. And the ones that aren't willing to go along, ya lure them into places like this by whatever means it takes."

"So what?" The wizard of deception starts playing, hoping to convince Joe to take up the fight once again. Cornelius soon quits. "Come on, kid, let's go! What are ya waiting for?"

"It's about the notes and what's between the notes," Joe answers in a moment of revelation. "They're the glue that holds everything together. That's what you're trying to rip apart."

"Look, if you're tired and ya really need a break, I'm okay with that. I can wait. There's no rush."

"No, I don't need a break." Joe declares with new resolve and energy.

"Well then, let's play damn it!"

"You're right. Let's play. I'm sorry for ya."

"Don't feel sorry for me," Cornelius answers coldly, his eyes narrowing to slits. "I'll lay a beating on ya that ya won't soon forget."

Joe seizes the initiative. At first his music sounds far off and lonely. Then he finds a clear, rich note sounding like a lost and dying man discovering a pool of water in a parched land. Immediately he knows the water was always there. New notes emerge into a song, calling to the tired and dispossessed. Offering refuge, his song gathers into a stream and then a clear cold river that grows in strength with each note.

Cornelius blasts his way in. The current is too strong for him. He's quickly exhausted and brushed aside into an eddy where he goes silent, unable to respond. He's no match for the song that is playing Joe.

And somewhere in his song, Joe finds Sally, Monk and Neil, and others who have cared and helped him on his journey. And the river turns into a bay and the bay into an ocean that empties into the stars and beyond the stars and beyond the galaxies and ripples out beyond the universe and beyond all that we know and surges into the wonders of vast uncharted realms.

Joe looks out over the spectators as he plays. Joki's seat is empty. He can't tell if she's stacked in one of the aisles. He can't stop playing to find her because his song is breathing new life into himself and the throng of listeners. Many of them are standing. Others are making their way to the exits. The TV screens are going dark.

Weakened by another lung-crushing, coughing fit, the lord of the lie staggers off stage. He shuts off all the Aud lights in a last desperate attempt to stop Joe. Cornelius is too late. Witnesses to Joe's song have thrown open the doors to the Aud. The light from the corridor floods the room, punching holes in the darkness.

Joe plays on like a musician possessed. Finally, the Aud doors silently close. Everyone has left, except Joe, who continues on until fully restored. He stops. The TVs are dead. The Aud is silent.

"Hello Joe," says a voice beside him in the dark. The voice is strong and warm. "It's me, Joki. It's been a long time. I missed you."

"How did ya find me?"

"I followed the music. Oh, I bumped into Cornelius running for the exit. He sounded like his hair was on fire.

He dropped this. He wouldn't stop to look for it. Here, you should have this." Fumbling in the dark, Joki hands the zapper to Joe.

"Thanks," says Joe, dropping it into his pocket. "Let's get out of here. I've had enough of this place."

"Yes, I'm with you."

B

A thick cloud of smoke swirls about Neil's head. He ignores the smoke, concentrating instead on the task at hand.

"I think it's ready. What do ya think?" he asks, holding up a charred hotdog on the end of a stick.

With his eyes tearing, Joe examines Neil's handiwork by the uneven light of the campfire. He blows out a couple of pesky flames.

Nearby stands a barn sufficient to house a Transit Jump. Neil found the unused barn in the middle of nowhere. He persuaded the owner, Everett Manjack, that he would make a good tenant despite his prior incarceration. Neil offered three bean-shaped objects to close the deal on the rental property. He explained that the beans had special properties. They would enhance the productivity of Everett's farmland, which is many counties distant from the rental property. Neil stated that he sought seclusion from prying eyes after his traumatic papier-mâché imprisonment.

Everett was suspicious of the farfetched tale of confinement. Nevertheless, after some shrewd calculations, and being a clever businessman, he accepted the beans. He decided that he didn't want to know the intended use of the barn. Deniability was the best strategy.

When Neil handed over the beans, he instructed Everett to plant them in separate corners of his farmland, as far away as possible from one another. Planting the beans together in the same spot would have dire consequences. Everett, who wasn't listening, nodded yes. Neil, for his part, was satisfied with the transaction, though a little wary of the laissez-faire attitude of his landlord.

"Yeah, it's ready," Joe concludes. "Not bad for a first try. Ya want me to fix it for ya?"

"Sure. Ya want one?"

"Okay. Maybe not so well done," Joe responds as he walks to a nearby table. He is glad to escape the smoke.

"What do ya want on it?"

"Surprise me."

Joe lays the hotdog in a bun and liberally applies mustard, relish, ketchup and onions. Returning to the campfire and doing his best to avoid the obstinate smoke, he carefully hands the gastronomic masterpiece to Neil. In exchange, Neil hands a hotdog on a stick to Joe, as though passing a baton.

"That's better, not quite so black," says Joe, examining Neil's latest effort. "You're getting the hang of it."

Neil looks doubtfully at Joe's gourmet effort. "You're sure this is how it's done?"

"Yep, all ya have to do is wrap your teeth around it, or whatever ya have that pass for teeth."

Carefully Neil brings the frankfurter to his mouth, trying not to let any of the condiments escape.

"It's best to start at one end," Joe points out, seeing that Neil is about to take a bite out of the middle.

"Does it matter which end?"

"Either end works. Trust me."

The smoke has again found Joe. He steps back a few paces from the fire.

Neil adjusts his hotdog and takes a bite. Without warning, Neil shakes violently, as if about to fly apart. Alarmed, Joe is uncertain what to do. Soon, Neil stops.

"Ya okay?"

"I'm fine. The smoke is a potential trigger for battlefield conditions. That plus the hotdog experience almost overwhelmed my Run program. My factory-installed programming tried to initiate. It's an unintended consequence of a new experience."

"Next time ya feel a reset coming on, let me know, will ya? I don't want to be anywhere near ya, if the old you makes an appearance. Maybe ya should ease up on new experiences for a while. Let your system adapt slowly."

"I'm alright now. I'm learning. I have to step out of my comfort zone, not give in to my old self."

"That sounds very human. I never thought that a hotdog could be so dangerous."

"It's like being a prisoner all your life and then set free. Suddenly there's a whole new world. That can feel threatening." Neil takes a second bite. "This is good! I like this." He alters the components of his face to manufacture a smile, hoping to ease Joe's concern. "Think I'll try another." He carefully impales a hotdog on a stick and eases it over the fire. "I'm getting the hang of this," he says, pleased with himself.

"You're like a little kid," Joe observes, smiling. "I think we made good progress today on the Transit Jump. What's your take on it?" he prompts, hoping for an update on the status of the engine. The technology is beyond Joe's understanding.

Neil carefully lays another piece of wood on the fire. He's oblivious to Joe's prompting.

Joe chokes back a cough. He waves his hand trying to fend off the smoke. "We can let the fire die down, if you've had enough."

"What about the marshmallows?" asks Neil, sounding a little worried that they might not be on tonight's menu.

"We can toast them over the coals."

A while later, having had their fill of marshmallows, Joe and Neil stare into the fire, enjoying the warmth and dance of the flames among the embers. Occasionally an errant breeze whispers encouragement to the fire, which softly gathers itself in ever diminishing responses. Not wanting the moment to end, Neil pokes the coals with a stick, temporarily encouraging the fire. The two of them sit in the quiet glow, lost in thought.

A chorus of frogs has started its nightly song. The night is clear. Overhead, countless stars fill the sky.

"I think we made good progress today," Joe prompts again, breaking the silence.

"I have a present for ya." Joe can hear Neil opening a compartment in his chest cavity. "Here," says Neil, handing Joe a scrap of cloth splattered with papier-mâché.

Joe holds it up to the failing light of the fire. He can make out a large B.

"It's part of your cape. Do ya remember? I tore it off at The Flour Mill. I like to think of it as a flag of victory."

"Ya went to prison. Where's the victory in that?"

"I found a new purpose in The Millhouse."

"What do ya want to do with the flag?"

"Let's hang it up in the barn as a reminder?"

"That's a good idea. Now I've got a question for you. How do I get rid of this?" Joe pulls Cornelius' zapper from his pocket and hands it to Neil. "I've tried to destroy it."

Neil is alarmed to see the zapper. "Ya can't. It's indestructible. The best I can do is hide it."

"Where?"

"Did Cornelius tell ya his story about the falcon and the crow?"

"What's that got to…"

"Never mind. I know a place. Trust me."

"Why don't ya take it with ya? Maybe ya could use it where you're going."

"Can't. Zappers are inherently unstable. It will throw off the calibration of the Transit Jump, if I try to take it with me. I don't know where I might end up. No place good I'm sure. How they managed to get it here, I don't know. It must have taken a great deal of effort. Besides, ya can't use it to force others. If ya do, ya construct a new hell in the name of Cornelius."

"Are ya going soon?"

188

"In a few days. I have most of the art stored in memory and there are only a couple of tests left to run on the Transit Jump. Why don't ya come with me? I don't mean right away. I have work to do at the other end first."

"I don't know," Joe responds, dumbfounded by the invitation.

"It's one thing to hear recorded music. It's another to hear and see a live performance that shows others what they can do, if they choose. They'd be hearing music in its natural state, an experience like no other, unadulterated. A recording isn't the same. A live performance can never be repeated. It's unique, like a fingerprint of who ya are in that moment of time. Wait a minute," says Neil opening another compartment. He pulls out a small cylinder. "Here," he says, handing it to Joe. "Careful with this."

Joe squints at the object. It's a small vial filled with a clear liquid. To get a better look, he holds it closer to the embers. In the center of the vial floats a tiny object no bigger than a kernel of wheat. Joe doesn't recognize it.

"Don't get it too close to the fire. I wouldn't want it damaged."

"What is this?"

"It's my real DNA. Everyone where I come from carries a vial like that."

"I don't get it. What's it for?"

"It's our right, the right to bear DNA. It's all that's left of me, my flesh and blood, my ancestry. The Tran leaders use it as propaganda to remind the Disposables what they're fighting for. Anything that we were once fighting for that might have been of value is gone. We changed into what ya see before you. We were told we needed to adapt to protect our civilization and what it represents: freedom. That wasn't true. We let others tell us who we are. It was a lie. They had their own agenda. We went along without thinking about the alterations we were making to ourselves. We poisoned our hearts and minds. And always when we made modifications, we said it would keep us free. Change became an honor and a duty to the Tran we served. We made sacrifices. We believed our sacrifices would keep us free. They didn't. They did the opposite. We were once much like you. If ya were to analyze my DNA, you'd find that it is much like yours," Neil lets the idea sink in. "What ya hold in your hand is all that's left, a token of what we once were, except for those at the top who control the Trans, ones like Cornelius. They created worlds in their own image and we let them."

After thinking for a moment about what Neil has said, a look of incredulity crosses Joe's face. "That makes ya a Frankenstein."

"That's right. Each of us is an assemblage of parts hammered together at the hands of our master. And that makes Cornelius...?"

"Dr. Frankenstein," replies Joe after a moment. "How long did it take ya to recognize him?"

"I recognized him when I first met him at BQT. I was confused at first. The official history of the Tran states that senior members of the Tran killed him long ago for crimes against the Tran."

"I thought that ya weren't good at facial recognition?"

"I'm not. He was easy to spot. The ideas he expressed betrayed him."

Neil utters a sound like that of an exploding grenade.

Joe covers his ears, stunned by the force. "What are ya trying to do? What was that?"

"That's an example of what passes for conversation where I come from."

"What did ya say?"

"Get Busy Dying."

The Unexpected

A family of barn owls look down from a barn rafter, curious about the activities below. Neil hovers over a set of controls mounted on a small panel. The panel sits on an old, wooden table to which he has attached the torn cape. The engine resides in the middle of the floor. It is not readily visible.

"The best way to see it is to use your peripheral vision," Neil advised, when he first showed the engine to Joe. "It takes practice. There are some people that never see. Their focus is too direct. They're blind in that sense; it's called focal dissonance. They choose to see only what is in front of them. There's also a phenomenon associated with the engine. If ya look at it in just the right way, ya can see a reflection of yourself. Some like what they see and some don't. What ya do with what ya see is another story."

There are no visible connections between the engine and the instrument panel. Neil once tried to explain it to Joe. He said the engine worked on the principle of Qlue, a kind of interconnectedness. His more detailed mathematical explanation was lost on Joe. And Neil had to admit that there was a point when even mathematics couldn't explain adequately.

"Hey Joe, play your sax, will ya?"

"Anything special?"

"You pick," says Neil, concentrating on the instrument panel.

Joe picks up his sax and, after a moment of thought, begins playing. He weaves through the music, enhancing it at every opportunity.

After about five minutes, Neil waves a hand, signaling that Joe can stop.

"How was that?"

"That was great. I haven't heard ya play that one before. What's it called?"

"*Mysterious Traveller*. It seems appropriate."

"Good choice. Okay, everything's set. I'm ready to go."

"Now, right now?" Joe is startled, even though he has known that this moment would come. Still, it's hard for him to accept.

"Yeah, now's as good a time as any. Before I go, there are some things about the Transit Jump that ya should know."

"I hope it doesn't involve Qlue and a lot of mathematics."

"No, nothing like that. It's ready. All I have to do is step in. The engine will do the rest. Once I go through, the controls will set to auto mode and lock. Ya won't be able to change them and ya wouldn't want to mess with them even if ya could. The settings are good for two years. It's powered by a green bean in the instrument panel. I didn't give all the beans to Everett. I kept one. After two years, the engine will start to degrade. Eventually, the instrument panel will implode and with it the engine. If ya want to join me, ya have two years to do it. I'm hoping ya will." Neil looks for a response from Joe, who shifts his weight uneasily. "I'm not sure I can explain why it's important that ya come. It's like that guy who sailed the seven seas. He found something that others need to know. It would be the adventure of several lifetimes crammed into one. We'd be explorers discovering new worlds. The Trans will try to stop us. It won't be an easy journey. What journey worth taking is easy?"

"How will I know if ya make it home?"

"Ya won't. There's no guarantee. I've arranged everything to the best of my ability."

"It's a big leap."

"Yeah. What will ya do if ya stay here? Ya could go back to Away Home Bay. Ya liked it there. It sounds like a nice place. Or maybe ya have another place in mind."

"What if I get to your world and don't like it? Maybe I get there and discover it's more of a challenge than I can handle. What then? Can I return here?"

"Best to think of it as a one-way ticket. I don't think you'll want to come back. We'll be too busy seeding the galaxies. I'm hoping you'll decide to step through. I could use your help. I appreciate that it's a huge decision. If ya choose not to come, I'll understand."

"I didn't get much sleep the last few nights thinking about it. I've decided I want to join you. I can't imagine a place without music, art, literature, film. What's the point without them? I want others to at least catch a glimpse of who they are, or could be. I want to be part of a bigger world."

Neil smiles. "Good."

"What's to stop someone else from stepping through?"

"Ya mean Cornelius? I've encrypted the engine. It will only respond to you and only when ya stand in it and play *Mysterious Traveller*. That's why I asked ya to play. I needed the music to set the engine for ya. It's dialed into your sax, your style of playing and *Mysterious Traveller*. It's like a fingerprint, unique."

"I was improvising. I can't play the piece again note for note."

"It doesn't matter. Play the music. It will work."

"What happens if someone else gets in the engine while I'm playing?"

"Won't work. It accepts only your DNA."

"How will I know when the engine is starting to degrade?"

"Watch the status light on the panel. Now it's green. When it turns amber, ya have a week to make the jump. Once it goes red, don't use it. And if it starts flashing red, get out. Ya don't want to be near it when it implodes. Ya could get pulled in. To be safe, ya should be outside the barn when it goes."

"Implode?"

"The Transit Jump will convert to a 'not Qlue state', for lack of a better explanation."

"How do ya know someone won't try to interfere with the panel, maybe take the green bean?"

"The panel has several layers of defense, if someone attempts to tamper with it."

"How will I know when you're ready at the other end and I can go through?"

"That's tricky. I won't be able to communicate with ya directly. The best I can do is send ya signs."

"Signs?"

"Yeah, signs," says Neil, sounding a little uncertain. "They may not seem like much and they may seem unrelated to one another. However, if ya put them together, you'll know that it's okay to join me. It's the best I can do."

"Sounds a little sketchy. How do I know that I'm not making stuff up? Ya know, misinterpreting things for signs that aren't. I could go nuts."

"You'll know. It'll feel right. I know it sounds vague. I'll try to narrow the field to make it easier. Read the Lickspittle," Neil adds. "Yeah, that's it. The signs will be there."

"Can ya give me a for instance?"

Neil thinks for a minute. "It's hard to explain. Look for items that on some level are related. Ya should practice looking for things that are common in some way, though it may not be evident at first. You're putting together the apparently unrelated to see something new. Ya may not understand right away. The new may be an intuitive understanding at first."

194

"Kind of like applying FS, Fearful Symmetry, to Qlue without relying on the mathematics."

"Yeah that's good way to think of it," Neil says enthusiastically, liking Joe's connection. "Maybe play the sax when you're looking for items. Ya want to see things differently, not in the way that you're used to looking at them. It takes practice. You'll figure it out."

"Anything else I should know?"

"That's it. The rent on this place is paid, though there won't be much to keep ya here once the machine exceeds its best-before date." Neil, hands a pair of welder's goggles to Joe. "You'll need this. The light will be very intense for a second when I step in."

"Ya got everything?"

"Yeah, the art and my DNA."

"What about the flag?"

"Bring it with ya when ya make the leap."

"Well, sounds like you're good to go," says Joe.

There's an awkward silence as the two of them try to think what remains to be said. Unexpectedly, Joe steps forward and hugs Neil. Taken aback, Neil at first returns the embrace awkwardly and then warms to the new experience.

"It's time," says Neil.

Joe puts on his goggles. He flashes a smile and gives a thumbs-up.

"Here goes." Neil steps into the engine. There's a flash of bright light.

Neil is gone.

Don't Know Beans

Joe stands vigil on the front porch of the farmhouse. The trees lining the laneway are beginning to bud. There is a pile of aging Lickspittle newspapers on a table beside him. His mail subscription to the paper offers a tenuous link to events in the outside world. From his vantage point, he watches the horizon for a cloud of dust. The mail truck is late, or maybe not coming today. Sometimes he can go for days without getting a newspaper. Often, he finds several editions stuffed in the mailbox when the mail does arrive. The papers are at least a week old by the time Joe receives them.

When a new copy arrives, Joe spends hours reading it in search of signs from Neil. He examines with a laser focus every word, letter and punctuation mark. There are the usual headlines: Indigenous Peoples Flee Pawsoff; Zombies Walk Among Us; Invasion Imminent; President Claims Rule by Divine Right; Religious Zealots Declare Might is Right; Prime Minister Suspends Parliament in Interest of Government Transparency; and Freedom Fighters Suspend Human Rights.

Sometimes, to pass the time while waiting for a fresh issue of the Lickspittle, Joe hunches over an old copy. As he reads, he plays his sax, exhorting the paper in some weird language to reveal any signs that he might have missed. The result is disappointing. He finds only sporadic grammatical and typographical errors. Joe used to agonize over these types of mistakes. Eventually, he accepted them for what they are, errors and not signs from Neil.

Taking a break from the newspaper, he spots in the distance a telltale plume of dust.

Mail truck? Joe speculates. *No, more likely someone lost.*

He has few visitors. Most who do reach the farm want directions. He resumes his reading.

A vehicle spins off the road and onto the farm laneway. Spitting gravel, it roars up the lane. The truck skids to a stop when Everett catches sight of Joe. The trailing column of dust catches up, enveloping the vehicle. Everett looks panicked. He hurriedly cranks open a window. He coughs, choking on the dust. Bending his body to his will, he stifles a coughing fit.

"Where's Neil?" he bellows, ignoring the strangeness of Joe playing his sax over a newspaper. "Is he in the barn? I need to talk to him now! There's a problem with the beans. Do ya know anything about beans?"

"No, I don't know beans," yells Joe.

"Is he in the barn?" shouts Everett.

Joe saunters over to the truck. Everett watches impatiently. He calculates how much money he is losing in the time it takes Joe to walk the dozen or so steps.

"Neil's gone."

"Gone! Gone where?" Everett shouts even though Joe is standing beside him. The veins on Everett's neck stick out. His face is choke-cherry red. His eyes bulge like angry volcanoes about to erupt. He's afraid to draw breath for fear that he will invoke more coughing. His head looks like it's ready to explode.

"Up there," answers Joe, looking skyward.

"Ya mean he's on a plane somewhere? Ya don't mean he's dead, do ya? The beans he gave me are ruining me! Where's he at?"

"Ya didn't plant them all in the same spot, did ya? Neil said not to do that."

"They're destroying everything!"

"He's gone home."

"Home where?"

"Back to his home world."

"Well call him up! Get him back here before I lose my farm! Someone has to answer for this!"

"There's no way to reach him and there's no way he can come back even if he wanted to."

"Never rent to an alien! Ya can't trust them! The truth is ya can't trust anyone," Everett angrily concludes, looking directly at Joe. "Who's going to pay for the damage, you? Never mind! If ya hear from him, tell him I'm looking for him."

Everett slams the truck into reverse and, swerving from side to side, retreats down the lane. He whirls onto the country road, narrowly missing the ditch, and races away at the speed of a missile. Dust billows in his wake.

Unconcerned, Joe casually returns to the porch. With no sign of the mail truck, he makes his daily pilgrimage to the barn where he checks on the Transit Jump. The green light on the control panel shines brightly. Two adult barn owls are raising a new brood of chicks. Everything looks fine.

Joe's routine remains unvaried. When not going about his daily chores, he plays his sax. Sometimes in the late evening, he has a campfire. It isn't the same without Neil. Late at night, he writes in his journal. If he hasn't seen the mail truck in a week, he drives a battered, pickup truck to the nearest village to make sure that the rest of the world hasn't wandered off, and to pick up supplies. Spring slips into summer. The owls successfully raise their brood. Everett does not re-appear. Joe wonders how Everett made out. He watches the Lickspittle for news.

Signs

Summer turns into fall, winter, and again into spring. Curiously, the owls do not return. Joe has moved his library of yellowing newspapers into the barn. A large stack of papers rests on the table beside the control panel. He carefully re-reads the old copies, looking for a sign from Neil. He plays his sax. He's worried that time is running out. Neil left almost two years ago. When Joe first started getting the paper, he was excited at the prospect of discovering signs from Neil. Now Joe grows increasingly worried with each new edition of the newspaper. He is concerned that he may have missed something. There are other possibilities too: Neil didn't make it home; his old programming kicked in; or he was captured by a Tran and reconstituted.

Then one day, Joe receives a letter from the Lickspittle. Due to declining readership, the newspaper will cease publication later this month. Even the Lickspittle is not immune to the inscrutable scramble of getting and spending.

Shortly after receiving the letter, Joe retrieves a lone copy of the Lickspittle from his mailbox. Emblazoned in large type on the front page are the words Final Edition. With his head immersed in the paper, he leafs through the pages during his walk to the barn. He stops, stunned by a small news article.

Former Lorean Businessman Returns

Cornelius Millhouse, a former major influence in the commercial development of Lore and many other communities both nationally and internationally, has temporarily returned to Lore. The reclusive owner of Millhouse Enterprises, and now a major industrial leader in the emerging economy of Pawsoff, is seeking a lost artifact. The item disappeared during the transition of his headquarters to Pawsoff. He has narrowed his search to a rural community several hours distant from Lore. Citing business confidentiality, Mr. Millhouse would not reveal the name of the community, or the nature of the missing object.

Said Clayton Pitts, the federal government's newly appointed Regional Development Officer, 'We are happy to assist Mr. Millhouse in any way possible.'

Joe glances at the date on the paper. It's a week old.

In the barn, the control panel's green light turned amber two days ago. Placing the paper on the table, he nervously rifles through the pages. There's still nothing. Discouraged and uncertain what to do, he picks up his sax and begins playing. Uncharacteristically, he turns his back on the paper as he plays. After a few minutes and forgetting his concerns, he travels through the music, following where it leads him. He stops. Excited, he thumbs through the paper, stopping briefly to re-read several headlines.

Scattered among the advertisements for weight loss, hair removal and other transformational products, Joe finds in the headlines the signs that have eluded him: Alien Runner Escapes Death; Former Millhouse Inmate Opens Art Exhibit; Sailor Presumed Drowned Found Alive;

Musician Raptures Audience; and Mysterious Traveler Disappears.

"That's it!" says Joe, feeling a great sense of relief. "He's cutting it close."

"Who's cutting what close?"

Joe whirls around, his heart racing like a runaway train.

"Good to see ya, kid. I guess ya didn't hear me come in. Is this what I think it is? Looks like a control panel for a Transit Jump." Cornelius moves casually to the front of the table. "Where's the Disposable?"

"Gone."

"That's too bad. I could've used it."

"How did ya find me?"

"The Lickspittle had your mailing address on file. I have to admit, you're a long way off the beaten path." Cornelius examines the control panel. "He used this to go home, didn't he? Where's the rest of it?" he demands, glancing about the barn.

Joe realizes Cornelius can't see the engine. He's astonished by Cornelius' blindness. Joe assumes that everyone can see it as easily as he does.

"If the panel is here, the engine must be here too. Why didn't the Disposable destroy it? All the unit had to do was set up an auto-destruct. This makes no sense. It must have known the danger of …" Cornelius ponders for a moment. "Well, who knew? The Disposable is waiting for ya, isn't it?" He glances at the controls. "Why haven't ya left? What's keeping ya here? Looks like you're almost out of time," he observes. "You're cutting it close. Where is it?"

"It's there. You're standing beside it."

"Where?"

"There," says Joe, pointing at the floorboards. "Stand on that knothole."

"Don't play with me. They're plenty of knotholes. Which one is it?"

"That one there, a few steps to your right," Joe directs. He smiles, knowing that he has the upper hand.

Cornelius grins. "Thanks. You're too honest. It's been nice knowing ya." He steps into the engine and waits. Nothing happens. "This thing busted?" he sputters. He steps out. "Is that why you're still here? Why are ya bothering with all the papers anyway? And what the hell is this rag?" he demands, ripping the scrap of cape from the table. "B? B what? Have ya gone nuts out here?" He throws the remnant at Joe's feet.

"It's a polishing cloth. I use it on my sax," Joe answers. He casually picks up the relic and stuffs it in his shirt. "And the machine is encrypted. It will only work for me."

"It looks like you're coming with me." He reaches across the table, grabs Joe's arm and pulls him toward the engine.

"No, ya don't get it. The machine doesn't work that way. It won't work for ya. I'm the only one. It's uniquely patterned for me."

Fuming, Cornelius looks like he is about to detonate. He releases Joe.

"I'm pulling the plug on this. I need time to figure this out."

"I wouldn't do that. It's not safe." Joe grabs his welding goggles and puts them on.

Cornelius examines the control panel. He flips a latch opening a compartment. "Well, look at that, my zapper! Life doesn't get any better, does it? Don't run off. I got plans for ya. What's with the glasses? They won't protect ya."

Joe is alarmed by how easily the master thief opened the panel, despite its defenses.

"I wouldn't touch anything," Joe warns, stepping into the engine.

Cornelius lunges for the zapper.

Joe launches into *Mysterious Traveller*.

News

"In local news today, there were unusual events at a remote farm north of the abandoned city of Lore", begins Sam, the TV news anchor. "We have our newest member of the team, Tom Booker, standing by on site. Over to you Tom."

"Thanks Sam. I'm standing here in front of a barn where earlier today I met with Cornelius Millhouse. Mr. Millhouse is a former, long-time resident of Lore and influential industrialist. I had arranged an interview with him regarding a lost artifact, the nature of which he would not divulge. He claimed to have found the location of the article. If successful in recovering the item, he stated that he would make an announcement later today about a major geopolitical realignment to resolve on-going tensions in Pawsoff. He insisted that I wait outside while he went into the barn. As Mr. Millhouse approached the building, I could hear music coming from inside. I captured the following events on camera. Roll the video please. Here's Mr. Millhouse entering the structure," Tom continues, while the video plays. "After several minutes, there is a burst of intense light that you can see between the barn boards. Almost immediately after, there is a loud noise and an inrush of air at high velocity that, even from where I was standing, I could feel. The entire event lasted only a few seconds. Later, I entered the barn. I could find no trace of Mr. Millhouse."

There is an interior shot of the barn. The control panel is gone and with it the engine.

"The cause of the phenomenon is unknown. When contacted by phone, the owner of the property, Everett Manjack, who refused to be interviewed on camera, would only say that he had rented the farm to Disposal-Man some time ago and that there had been little contact since. You may remember an item that the news team brought you last year regarding Mr. Manjack. At the time, he was embroiled in a firestorm of legal battles, regarding another rural property he owns. And you may remember Disposal-Man, an extraterrestrial being, who served time in The Millhouse for destruction of private property. Police are continuing their investigation regarding Mr. Millhouse's inexplicable disappearance. Back to you Sam."

"Thanks Tom. We look forward to hearing more on this story in the coming days. In international news, events in Pawsoff are spiraling out of control as the country plummets into chaos. There are escalating armed clashes between rival groups vying for control of the lucrative, coal industry. The government of Pawsoff in recent years has opened the coal fields to development by international business consortiums after enormous pressure by political and commercial interests. We have this video that shows the growing violence in…"

RT

Joe removes his welder's goggles. The sun shines dimly through the brown pall of the gritty, choking atmosphere. He stands on a metal plate that spans countless hectares. It is one of almost numberless interconnected plates that stretch in all directions, forming a skin over the entire planet. In the distance, Joe can make out the spires of a massive industrial complex that extends unbroken as far as he can see. Behind the complex, looms the vague shape of a full moon partially cloaked by the atmosphere.

"Ya made it!"

Joe turns in the direction of the voice.

"Neil!" says Joe, happy to see him.

"Good to see ya," says Neil, hugging Joe. "I thought maybe ya changed your mind."

"Almost didn't make it. Cornelius showed up."

"And?"

"Last I saw, he was reaching for his zapper. I thought ya said the control panel had defenses? He opened it like a kid opening a piggy bank."

"I realized he might find the Transit Jump and the zapper. I set it up so that he was the only one who could open the panel. When he removed the zapper, it caused an implosion. I had hoped ya would've made the jump sooner. I had difficulty getting my message through, but ya made it," declares Neil. "That's what counts."

"What happened to Cornelius?"

"He was sucked in by the implosion. It was the only way I could hope to get rid of the zapper and Cornelius at the same time."

"Is he gone for good?"

"No."

"Where is he now?"

"Don't know. He's out there somewhere and still has the zapper. He won't be bothering us for a while. Are you still going by the name Joe?"

"Yeah," Joe answers. "It's time for a new name." Joe thinks for a minute. "Jeremiah, call me Jeremiah."

"Why Jeremiah?"

"A wise man once said, 'she's easy to loose'. He was right."

"What's easy to loose?"

"Language, and the way we say things. I like to think he was talking about how easy it is to forget who we are. We're strangers to ourselves doing the bidding of others for their own bizarre ends."

"Serving strange gods in a land that is not yours," says Neil, scanning the horizon.

"How is your Run program holding up?" Jeremiah asks, remembering Neil's struggle the night of the hotdog feast.

"I've improved it. It's less susceptible to a factory reset, if that's what you're asking. I renamed it RT."

"RT?"

"Run True. Come on. We're exposed here. The Trans have banded together. They're moving against us. I've made some inroads. We have a lot of work to do. Are ya ready to run?"

Glossary

AI – Apathy and Ignorance
Aud – Auditorium
BiCS – Best in Class Speak
BIFem – Better Integrate Family Members
BQT – Buzz Quick Time Co.
BQTaH – BQT at Home
BQTer – BQT Employee
BRD – Basic Rights Document
BtR – Buy the Rights
CcP – Cross-Culture Pollination
CKM – Cornelius Krissen Millhouse
CMO – Chief Minimalist Officer
CPers – Crap Police
CRD – Component Replacement Depot
CtC – Cut the Crap
DB – Dead Balls
DDWE – see DDWEwtE
DDWEwtE – Damage Done While Engaged with the Enemy
DeCom – Decommissioning
DED – Dog Eat Dog
DGT – Don't Go There
DLS – Distracted Living Syndrome
DNA – Dynamic Nomenclature Authentication
DTs – Domestic Terms
DV – Domestic Version
EA – Economic Advancement
EnFs – Employees and Families

FerS –Disposables that use FS
FnE – Flourish and Evolve
FQ – Fiscal Quarter
FS – Fearful Symmetry
FTS – Forget That Shit
GBD – Get Busy Dying
GPDA – General-Purpose Disposable Asset
GTL – Global Thought Leader
IIABDFI – If It Ain't Broke Don't Fix It
IF – Imaginative Focus
JT – Jingo Talker
LGC – Liberty Guard Corp. Ltd.
LNTB – Leave No Turds Behind
LoCR – Letter of Crap Reprimand
MAAIU – Mission Assignable Actively Independent Unit
MCI – Major Conflict Interjection (a war)
ME – Millhouse Enterprises
MIUaUG – Make It Up as You Go
NBs – Newbies
NMCfU – No More Crap from You
NoMoHo – No Mourning or Honoring
NPA – National Protection Agency
NR – No Rules
OG – Official Glossary
OTnot – Ought Not
OTnotS – OTnot Speak
OTs – Old Timers
PDVS – Post Dramatic Villain Syndrome
Pho – Photographer
PJC – Pro-tran Jingo Crew
PJCers – Pro-tran Jingo Crew members
RC – Resource Choke
RE – Receiving Elevator
Reconned – Reconstituted
RT – Run True
SA – Situational Awareness
SB – ScuttleButt

SFoD – Stay Free or Die
SM – Senior Management
SMEs – Subject Matter Experts
SnC – Spouses and Children
ST – Speak Think
SV – Super Villain
T3 – Tier Three (a superhero classification)
TC – Tran Commerce
TGC – Trans Galactic Conglomernation (Tran)
TLs – Thought Leaders
ToSh – Tough Shit
Tran – Trans Galactic Conglomernation
UPT – United People's Testament
WiP – Work in Progress
WS – We're Screwed
W'sYerP – What's Your Point?
YerT – You're Trespassing
YHNBbH – You Have No Business Being Here

Manufactured by Amazon.ca
Acheson, AB

11466471R00120